12-03 OX / Never OCT 2 6 2004 CR✓

A Killing in
Plymouth Colony

Carol Otis Hurst
Rebecca Otis

Houghton Mifflin Company Boston 2003

Walter Lorraine Books

Walter Lorraine (wл) Books

www.houghtonmifflinbooks.com

Library of Congress Cataloging-in-Publication Data
Hurst, Carol Otis.
  A killing in Plymouth Colony / Carol Otis Hurst & Rebecca Otis.
    p. cm.
Summary: In Plymouth Colony in the 1630s, John continually disappoints
his father, Governor William Bradford, during a difficult time as the
colony faces its first murder and subsequent trial.
  ISBN 0-618-27597-5
  1. Plymouth (Mass.)—History—17th century—Juvenile fiction. [1.
Plymouth (Mass.)—History—17th century—Fiction. 2. Bradford, William,
1588–1657—Fiction. 3. Fathers and sons—Fiction. 4. Murder—Fiction. 5.
Puritans—Fiction. 6. Frontier and pioneer life—Massachusetts—Fiction.] I.
Otis, Rebecca. II. Title.
  PZ7.H95678Ki 2003
  [Fic]—dc21
                                                    2002156429
Printed in the United States of America
MP 10 9 8 7 6 5 4 3 2 1

CONTENTS

Cast of Characters

John Bradford: Eleven-year-old son of the governor of Plymouth Colony.

Governor William Bradford: Second governor of the colony. Father of John, Young William, and Mercy. Husband of Alice.

Alice Southworth Bradford: Second wife of William Bradford. Stepmother to John, mother of Young William and Mercy.

Samuel Eaton: Best friend of John Bradford, brother of Rachel.

Rachel Eaton: Five-year-old sister of Samuel.

Francis Eaton: Carpenter. Father of Samuel and Rachel.

Christine Penn Eaton: Stepmother of Samuel. Mother of Rachel.

John Billington: Freeman of Plymouth. Seen by Bradford as a troublemaker.

Samuel Fuller: Physician for the colony.

Bridget Fuller: Midwife and wife of Samuel.

William Brewster: Elder of the church. Father figure to the governor.

Thomas Morton: One of the people who came to New England to profit from the trading industry.

John Alden: Barrel maker. Freeman of Plymouth.

Priscilla Mullins Alden: Wife of John.

Isaac Allerton: First assistant to Governor Bradford and a tailor.

Miles Standish: Captain, head of the militia in Plymouth.

John Howland: Former servant. Freeman of Plymouth.

Elizabeth Howland: Wife of John Howland.

John Newcomen: Single man, one of the later arrivals in Plymouth.

Edward Doty: Bondservant to the Hopkins family.

Reverend Smith: Pastor of the church.

The Kempton Family: Ephraim, Julia (sister of Alice Bradford), and their four children. They live in the Bradford house.

Thomas Clarke: Colonist assigned to the Aptucxet trading post.

Massasoit: Leader of the Wampanoags. A great and powerful ally of the Pilgrims.

Hobbamuck: One of Massasoit's counselors, living near the Pilgrim village with his family to serve as translator and keep Massasoit informed.

Preface

In Central America, the Spanish had been ruling the Aztecs since 1521. In England, William Shakespeare died in 1616. In America, a European epidemic reached what is now eastern Massachusetts, killing large portions of the native population in 1618. In China, Emperor T'ien-ch'i of the Ming dynasty had just begun his reign in 1620.

Also in 1620, John's father and mother boarded a crowded ship in Holland and traveled across the Atlantic Ocean on the *Mayflower*. With them were about forty members of their congregation. About sixty others from England, who were coming to America for other reasons, joined them. All were starting a new life.

In England, only one religious belief was allowed. John's parents and their congregation felt that the Church of England had strayed too far from the original Christian church. Because of their beliefs, they and many others had left England and lived in Holland for twelve years. Now they wanted a community of their own, where their children could still be English and where the official church would be their church.

John, only one year old at the time, was left behind in Holland with others in the congregation while his parents went to start the new colony.

It was November and getting cold when they anchored off the shore of Cape Cod, Massachusetts.

John's mother fell overboard and drowned, her new life ending before it had begun.

John's father and the others built a common house and a few small huts, making do as best they could. That first harsh winter, illness, exposure, and malnutrition killed half of them. The people must have wondered if God had found them unworthy. In April, Governor Carver died. John's father, William Bradford, was elected governor.

After that first terrible winter, their colony improved. In 1623, John's father wrote to Alice Southworth in Holland, asking her to come and be his wife. Five-year-old John stayed in Holland with the family that had been taking care of him, but Alice came and married John's father.

The people in Plymouth needed to pay the men in England who had financed their trip. They set up trading posts to get furs from the Indians along the coast, from what is now Maine all the way to the Connecticut River.

More settlers had come to Massachusetts Bay Colony, to the north, so the Pilgrims had a new market for their livestock and other goods.

Times were changing; the people of Plymouth were moving farther away from the central village into what would become other towns in the colony.

In 1628, John Bradford himself boarded a crowded ship and crossed the Atlantic to join the grand adventure.

All the above is true. The rest of this book is fiction. It takes place in 1630. John Bradford has been in the colony for two years.

The story is based on real people who lived in Plymouth in 1630, and as much factual information as we could find. But it is a story. We don't know what John Bradford was really feeling when he came to live with his family after eight years away from his father and with his mother dead. We don't know many details about the killing.

This is our idea of what might have happened.

1

Spy

That morning, the wind blew so strong from the sea that even the hardy sea gulls took shelter. They sat now in the cove, facing away from the wind, making a pattern of gray and white against the darker gray of the rocks beneath.

Like the sea gulls, Samuel Eaton and John Bradford kept their backs to the wind as they worked on top of the hill overlooking the cove. They hoped to finish splitting kindling for their families quickly and find some indoor chores near the fire for the rest of the day.

Both nearly twelve, the boys worked and played together whenever they got the chance. Sam—an Old Comer—had been in Plymouth since the beginning, but he'd been quick to welcome John when he arrived two years ago. Plymouth Colony was growing, but even now, in 1630, there were few boys between the ages of ten and thirteen.

"Sam! Come quick! Help! She's hurt! Help me catch her!" Sam's sister, five-year-old Rachel, ran toward them waving her arms around frantically.

"Catch? Catch who? Who's hurt?" Sam yelled, but the wind carried his words away. The boys put down their axes and followed Rachel, who was already running back into the woods. One end of her blue cape trailed on the ground behind her. Her long green shift was torn all along the hem, and she stumbled a bit because, as usual, she forgot to lift her skirt when she ran.

The thin layer of snow crackled and squeaked under their shoes. Their breath cast small white clouds behind them. They slowed as Rachel did when she approached a thicket.

"Who is it?" Sam asked as they drew closer. "Who's been hurt? Shall I fetch Master Fuller?"

"Shhh!" she cautioned, her finger to her lips. Then she pointed. "There! See her? She's hurt. Help her, Sam!"

A small dark shape lunged and fluttered against the brittle branches within the clearing.

John shook his head as he turned to Sam. "Fie! 'Tis nothing but a cursèd crow," he said. "Come away."

"All this fuss over a crow? Leave it be, Rachel," Sam said. He turned to leave, but Rachel grabbed his arm.

"'Tis Spy! Help her, Sam!" she cried. Rachel turned to John with her hands on her hips. "She's not cursèd. She's one of God's creatures, and she's my pet."

"Pet? A crow's not a pet!" John snorted. "C'mon, Sam. There's work to be done."

"Crows are pests, Rachel," Sam said patiently. "They steal the corn, and they make such a racket in the woods, they scare off any animal in earshot. Take one of the lambs or a pig for a pet, like the other girls do."

Sam gave John a look that begged for understanding, and then glanced down at his sister's face. Sam and Rachel looked much alike. They had the same sandy-colored curly hair and bright blue eyes. Now Rachel's eyes were swimming with tears, and her lower lip trembled. "Aw, Rachel," Sam said. He knelt in front of his sister, wiping away with his thumb the tears that had begun to fall. With his other hand he straightened her coif.

"She's my pet, Sam." Rachel spoke in spurts between sobs. "She's almost tamed. She comes when I call. She takes food from my hand. She's hurt. She'll die, Sam. Help her."

"Hush now. Ye'll scare it to death with such chatter."

The deep voice startled the children, and they turned almost in unison to face its source. Master John Billington motioned for quiet as he approached the thicket.

The children glanced warily at one another. They all knew the man, of course. In the small colony of three hundred souls, there were no strangers, but the children were more than a little leery of Master Billington. All three had been told many times to stay away from the Billingtons. Yet here was one of them in their very midst.

The flapping inside the thicket increased as the already panicked bird caught sight of the approaching man.

"Oh, don't hurt her!" Rachel cried out.

Within seconds, Master Billington emerged from the thicket, holding the hurt bird gently in his hands. One wing hung down uselessly, while the other flapped in a frantic attempt to fly. He stroked the bird's head with one finger, avoiding the darting beak. Then he placed the angry crow into Rachel's outstretched hands.

"Now," he said, "hold to it like that, lass, but don't squeeze it. It won't like this much."

"'Tis all right, Spy," Rachel cooed, bringing her face down close to the bird. "'Tis going to be all right. This nice man is helping thee."

The crow tried again to bite as Master Billington's thumb and index finger touched the wing and moved to the break. He twisted his fingers suddenly, snapping the bone into place. The bird squawked once and then was still.

Keeping his fingers on the site of the break, Master Billington turned to John Bradford. "Find me a straight stick this big," he said, measuring a length between the thumb and forefinger of his free hand before taking out a handkerchief.

"Not here," he said scornfully as John scuffed the dirt near his feet. "Go where the sticks are, boy!" He waved the handkerchief toward a clump of trees at the edge of the clearing, and John scurried off. Master Billington handed the handkerchief to Samuel. "Tear me a strip," he said.

Using his teeth to begin the tear, Sam ripped free a strip of cloth and handed it to Master Billington. A moment later John was back with a small stick. Nodding to express his satisfaction, the man placed it against the break. He motioned for John to hold it in place. Keeping a wary eye on the bird's beak, John did so. Master Billington wrapped the cloth strip around the stick and wing, fastening the splint in place.

"Two more strips, boy," he said to Sam, and then used them to immobilize the wing against the bird's body.

Master Billington bent down close to Rachel and her injured pet. "Now comes the hard part, lass. That bird needs water and food, and it can scarce fetch for itself. See that it gets both, and it'll be right as rain in a few weeks." He paused. "I doubt it'll fly again."

He walked toward a path leading into a pine thicket and then turned back to the children. "Regards to yer fathers," he said with a grin, and as silently as he had come, he was gone.

"I love him," Rachel declared, looking after him.

"Thou don't love him. Thou hardly know him, Rachel," her brother scolded.

"I do too. I love Master Billington," Rachel said, a determined look on her face.

"Well, don't say that around Father. He's not likely to want to hear much good about any Billington."

"And surely not around *my* father," John Bradford said. "If he had his way, all three Billingtons would be exiled from the colony. He says they've been a torment to him from the beginning."

"I don't care," Rachel said, stroking the head of Spy with one finger as Master Billington had done. "He saved Spy, and I love him."

2

The Next Day

"John, thou shall work at Deacon Fuller's this morning on the beasthouse," Governor Bradford ordered the next morning. Like most of the men in the colony, the governor wore a doublet over his white linen shirt. His was dark green. His gray breeches reached to the knee where they met the long wool stockings. He put on his cloak, hat, and gloves and unlatched the door before turning to face John directly.

"And see that thou stay to the task this morning, John. I want no more reports of thy taking off to the woods when there's work to be done."

John struggled for the words to explain what had happened the day before, but before he could speak the wind snatched the door out of his father's hands. Smoke billowed from the hearth, and bits of ash flew about the room as the cold air swept in. His father stepped out, slammed the door behind him, and was gone.

John spooned the last of his porridge into his mouth and shook his head. It never ceased to amaze him that everything—*everything*—he did got back to his father. He and Sam had only been away for moments to see to that foolish crow, and they'd gone

back to work almost immediately. The kindling was
split and piled by noon, but someone had told the
governor that his son had left the work even for that
short while. Whoever it was must not have seen Master Billington helping them, or there would have been
harsher words this morning.

Most of the others in the household must already
be outside working, John thought. Like almost every
house in Plymouth, this one held not only the main
family, but many other people as well. Governor
Bradford, John's stepmother, and the two younger
children slept in one room on the main floor. His
stepmother's sister Julia Kempton and the other five
members of her family slept in this room, where the
cooking and eating went on during the day, and three
single men slept in the loft with John.

In Plymouth everyone was expected to work for the
good of the household and the community. Sharing
shelter was part of that work, but it made things difficult sometimes. There was scarcely room to breathe
when all were inside.

John hoped to add a small lean-to on to the side of
this room someday. Even that added small space
should help. He'd been saving leftover materials from
various building projects around the village. Sam's
father, who was a good carpenter, had been putting
aside a few bits of lumber for him as well. John

would soon have enough to begin construction.

"Dress warmly, John. 'Tis bitter cold still." His stepmother spoke over her shoulder as she helped three-year-old Mercy with her apron. Young William was still eating his porridge over by the hearth, the only source of warmth in the house.

John smiled and nodded. "Aye, Mother." Smiles were easy to come by around his stepmother. John loved her, and he knew that, to her, he was as dear as the children she herself had borne. John thought he could remember her from Holland, although she had left when he was only five. His father and own mother had left when he was a year old, so his father and he had been strangers to each other when John arrived two years ago. Indeed, John thought, it seemed as if they still were.

John remembered how it had been the day he came to Plymouth, confused and scared, stumbling about, trying to get his land legs, after weeks aboard the *Talbot*. Stepping out of the shallop, he had seen his new mother grinning, with wide-open arms, standing beside his father.

Try as he might, John couldn't remember anything his father had done or said that day, but things had been good between John and his stepmother from the beginning.

Now John said his goodbyes and opened the door.

Remembering his father's struggle, he kept tight hold as he stepped out, closing the door quickly behind him. He leaned there for a moment in the shelter of the house, bracing himself against the cold.

The Bradford house stood in the center of the village where The Street and The Highway crossed. There was nothing grand about the governor's house. In Plymouth Colony no family was supposed to be held in any higher regard than another—a fine thought, but everyone was not really treated the same way, John knew. Just look at the way people treated the Bradfords, the Fullers, and the Eatons. Then look at the way most of them treated the Billingtons.

At the top of the hill stood the meetinghouse. Church services were held there every Sunday. It had a gun deck on the top floor, which served as a lookout in case of trouble with the Indians or the Spanish. So far, praise be to God, there had been little need for the fort's protection or for the palisade fence that led from each side of it.

John served his time up there, as did every other male over the age of ten in the colony. He was glad that he did not have sentry duty this bitterly cold day, and he felt sorry for those who did.

Even after two years in the colony, John was often taken aback by the large expanses of land here. In Holland, where he'd lived the first ten years of his life, most of the land was taken. The streets were filled with people, and there were shops everywhere. How nice it would be now to go into a shop and buy what he needed, instead of waiting for months for it to arrive by ship or, more likely, making do without it.

So many things had been different in Holland. There he'd been treated like a child. He had often resented that, but at least he was allowed time for play. Here work filled every day, except for the Sabbath, of course, when no one worked. And here he was the son of the governor, and that was the hardest work of all.

This morning there was the beasthouse to build. At least John would be at the Fullers and, likely, he'd be working with Sam. Most days each boy had to work for his own household either in the village or the fields. Days when they could work or play together, even for brief periods, were treasured.

Because Master Fuller was the physician for the community, and Goodwife Fuller acted as midwife, people repaid them by doing things the Fullers didn't have time to do, and today it was working on their beasthouse.

John would much rather go with Sam through the fields this morning—maybe scare up a rabbit or a turkey. Still, in this cold, probably no creature would be about that didn't have to be. John sighed, pulled his hat down over his ears, drew his cloak tighter, and headed down the hill toward the Fuller house.

John and Sam rived all morning, making clapboards by pounding the froe with a mallet into the log until the thin boards split off. It was hard work, and they took turns, one pounding the mallet while the other held the froe. John kept his eye on the pile of clapboards, hoping there'd be a few left over for his lean-to.

At least there was some shelter from the wind, thanks to the fence on the windward side of the Fuller garden that he and Sam had put up last fall. Even so, the sharp cold cut through them. Usually the two friends talked when they had a chance to work together. Other than his stepmother, Sam was the only person in Plymouth whom John felt he could talk to, but it was too cold this morning for conversation. They warmed their hands under their cloaks frequently and were grateful when Goodwife Fuller called them in at noonday.

Rachel was seated by the fire, sharing her meal with Spy, who perched on her shoulder, the white of the bandage stark against the bird's shiny black feathers.

". . . and Master Billington handed his handkerchief to Sam and told him to tear it," she was saying as they entered. "Master Billington's very own handkerchief." She shook her head at the wonder of it.

Both boys looked quickly at Goody Fuller, who was calmly dishing out their pottage. She seemed not the least bit disturbed to hear the Billington name uttered in her household. Still, such conversation made the boys nervous. John filled his cup with milk with an unsteady hand.

"Spy seems to be used to her bandage, Rachel," Sam said, trying to distract his sister.

Rachel smiled and nodded. "Spy would have died if Master Billington hadn't helped," she went on between sips of milk. "Master Billington knows everything about crows and broken wings. He's very kind. I love him."

Goodwife Fuller smiled fondly at her youngest guest and then turned to the boys. "How's the work?" she asked. "Will the beasthouse be ready soon?"

Both boys nodded enthusiastically, relieved at the change of subject.

"We'll soon be finished with the clapboards, I think," Sam said. "It should be ready by the end of the week."

Rachel broke off a piece of her johnnycake, soaked it in milk, and held it out to Spy, who gulped it down and poked at her hand for more.

"Master Billington says crows can learn to talk. I'm going to teach Spy to talk," Rachel said. "Master Billington's going to show me how. Say 'Rachel,' Spy," she said. "Rachel . . . Rachel. Come on, Spy. Say it." The bird stared at her, opening and closing its beak soundlessly. Rachel nodded encouragingly and then turned back to Goodwife Fuller. "Master Billington says it will take some time," she explained.

"Master Billington said nothing of the sort," Sam said. "Stop telling tales, Rachel."

Rachel jumped up from the bench. The bird flapped its good wing, barely managing to keep its footing on her shoulder. "I'm not telling tales, Sam! Master Billington said so this very morning. Thou weren't even there. Thou know nothing about it!"

Sam and John glanced quickly at each other. They hurriedly downed their dinners and rushed back to work. Not even the warmth of the fire could tempt them to stay around for more such talk.

3

Hunting

Later that week John and Sam went hunting at first light. Neither was a very good shot, but they did sometimes succeed in bringing down a bird or two.

The wind had let up a bit, and the cold seemed more bearable than it had been the last few days. They crossed the planting fields, keeping a sharp eye out for turkeys or quail.

The fields were covered with snow now, but come spring they'd be planted with beans, corn, and other crops. Each colonist who had arrived at Plymouth on the first three ships had been given one acre of planting field at the beginning. Three years ago these First Comers had been given even more land.

At the edge of the farthest field, Sam and John turned and walked slowly along the edge of the woods, where bushes sometimes served as shelter for game.

"Did Rachel tell thy mother and father about Master Billington helping Spy?" John asked.

"Aye, and it earned her another lecture." Sam used his gun to push away the thick branches of a bush. "I doubt it did much good, though," he said. "Thou know how Rachel is."

"Why is everyone so bothered about Master

Billington?" John asked. "I don't know him well, but he was nice to Rachel."

They walked along slowly, enjoying the time away from regular chores.

"He's a strange one," Sam said. "Nice enough when he's sober, but when he's drunk, watch out. He argues a lot at freemen's meetings, Father says." Sam chuckled a bit. "I guess the Billington family has been trouble since the beginning. They've all been put in the stocks at one time or another. They had a son who died just before thou came. He almost set fire to the *Mayflower* when it lay at anchor, my father says."

John shook his head. "And didn't their other son get in trouble with Massasoit?"

"Aye. He ran off, got lost, and Massasoit had to have his men bring him back. And Father says Master Billington was connected to the Oldham Conspiracy back in 1624, but they couldn't prove anything. They nearly tied him feet to neck once for blasphemy against Captain Standish, but Billington pled for mercy. He's a thorn in thy father's side, I guess."

John nodded. "Father has nothing good to say about the man."

"Have thou ever seen Billington drunk?"

"No, have thou?"

"Aye," Sam said. "I was on sentry duty a few

months ago and saw him come staggering up The Street." Sam laughed. "There was a group of women standing there. I couldn't hear what he said to them, but it surely upset them. Then, when they were all still looking at him, he relieved himself. Right in the street! You should have seen the women then."

John laughed. "I wager the group broke up quickly."

"Aye," Sam said. "I shouldn't laugh, I suppose, but it was funny."

"What would make a man drink till he's senseless?" John asked.

Sam shrugged. They walked on to the next thicket. A rabbit scampered out, but was gone by the time they could aim at it.

"We'll have to be quicker than that," Sam said. "Does thy father talk about Billington much?"

John laughed. "He has a lot to say about him." He turned toward his friend. "Not to me. Father seldom speaks to me, except to give me orders. He tells the others at home about the meetings, where Billington opposes him on almost everything."

"Why is that, does thou think?"

"Why does Billington oppose Father?"

"No," Sam said. "Why doesn't thy father talk to thee?"

"Does thy father talk to thee?" John asked.

"Of course," Sam said.

"Apart from lessons, I mean."

"Aye, he talks to me."

"What about?"

Sam shrugged. "I don't know. This and that. About what went on during freemen's meetings. About growing up in Yorkshire. About having to leave England. Thou know."

John shook his head. "That's just it, Sam. I don't know. My father speaks to me only when absolutely necessary or during lessons. I've been here two years, Sam. Thou would think he'd be used to me by now."

"I wonder why they left thee behind in Holland. My parents brought me, and we're the same age."

John shrugged. "I know. One year old and they put me with strangers."

"Not strangers, John. They put you with Reverend Robinson and his family."

John nodded. "Might as well have been strangers. I wouldn't have been that much trouble, would I? For years I thought there must be something wrong with me—that somehow they knew I wasn't one of the Chosen Ones. Maybe I'm not." His breath caught, and he swallowed hard before he went on. "Then my own mother died as soon as they got here. Maybe, if she'd lived . . ." He drew a deep breath. "All those years in Holland, waiting. I thought he'd just forgotten I existed. Sometimes I think he still forgets even when I'm under his nose. It makes it really hard, Sam. If it weren't for thee and Mother . . ."

There was a rustling noise in the next bush, and a large bird took flight a few yards in front of them. Both boys aimed and fired, but the bird flew on.

"Fie!" John said. "Neither of us can hit the broadside of a beasthouse from a foot away."

Sam grinned as they lowered their fowling pieces and walked on.

"My father's a hard man, Sam," John said. He never would have dared to say such a thing to anyone but Sam.

"Oh, I don't think so," Sam protested. "Thou should have seen him when my father was sick a few years ago, John. Your father was there every day and many nights to give my mother some relief. She says she never would have made it without him. People truly respect thy father, John. They elect him governor year after year."

John nodded. "Aye," he said. "People like him. And I know he's brought this colony through the hard years. In Holland we heard all about it. Reverend Robinson talked about my father a lot. I was so proud of him, Sam. I couldn't wait to see him, to know him. But he speaks at length to me only during lessons—about the ideas in the books, about the meaning of the passages in the Bible, but never about personal things. Now I'm living in the same house with him at last, and I still don't know him."

He poked his gun into another bush.

"He's soft with Mercy and Young Will," John went on. "And it's clear that he loves them. He plays with them, hugs them even." He turned to look straight at Sam. "But with me, 'tis different, Sam. He looks from them to me, and his smile disappears."

They stopped as they came to the rise overlooking the shore.

John turned to Sam again. "I waited so long to come here, Sam. Every letter that came, I hoped it would bring word from him for me to come. I prayed night and day for God to will him to send for me."

"That must have been hard."

"He sent for Mother years before he sent for me, Sam. He wanted a new wife before he wanted me. His own son!"

Sam nodded glumly. He could think of nothing to say that would cheer his friend.

"When I finally got the letter asking me to come two years ago," John went on, "I was so happy I danced in the street. I thought I'd be part of a real family at last."

"Well, thou art part of a real family," Sam said, glad to be able to say something positive. "Thou have a stepmother most in the village would envy, and Young Will and Mercy and thy father. Thou art, after all, his eldest son. He's proud of thee, John; he must be."

John shook his head. "I might as well be a stranger's son. Nothing I do is good enough. Everything I say is wrong." He turned and walked ahead, not wanting Sam to see the tears in his eyes.

He wiped them away quickly as a quail fluttered up from the thicket, followed by two more. Both boys fired and two birds fell.

4

Thomas Morton

Everyone in Plymouth seemed to be on The Street on a brisk March afternoon as John came up the hill from where he'd been splitting firewood with Ed Doty, servant to the Hopkins family. John hoped to meet up with Sam and do some fishing that evening.

People were clustered in small groups along the street, all talking at once, and John couldn't make out what they were saying. He'd have to wait for the evening meal to hear about the meeting that must have just ended.

What went on at the freemen's meetings was usually of little interest to John, but this one must have been exciting. They were to have decided what to do about Thomas Morton. Morton was not a citizen of Plymouth, but he was certainly a familiar and controversial figure here.

In 1628, the year John had arrived in Plymouth, Morton had been accused of a crime against the Crown—selling guns to the Indians. John's first night in Plymouth, much of the talk at the evening meal had been about Thomas Morton.

Soon afterward, Morton had been found guilty, exiled, and sent back to England. The people of Plymouth had been so anxious to get rid of Morton that they had taken him out to an island in the harbor to await the next ship. And that was supposed to have been the last of him, but Thomas Morton had recently come back to Plymouth, the guest of Isaac Allerton, and he was almost immediately in trouble again.

"Bold as brass, he was," the governor said that evening at supper as he dipped his bread into the trencher to soak up more broth. "There's no shame in the man." He took a sip of beer and then set the bowl beside him on the bench before picking up his spoon. Just then one of the Kempton children hit against the bench while walking through the room, spilling beer all over the rushes on the floor. The governor glanced quickly at Young William, who took the bowl and refilled it, setting it carefully back on the table.

"What charges were brought against him this time?" Goody Kempton asked.

John's stepmother turned to her youngest son. "Eat up, Young William."

"Indeed," said the governor, smiling at his younger son. "Thy mother's a good cook, Young Will. Don't miss any of it."

John, seated on a barrel near the hearth, waited for the usual lecture about the people who died that first winter in Plymouth. His father usually gave it whenever anyone threatened to leave food uneaten, but the governor's mind was on Morton. He turned back to the others.

"He's wanted for suspicion of murder back in England, and he's already causing trouble here."

"Who spoke against him?" Goody Kempton asked.

"Most of the Old Comers. And John Newcomen. But what does he know? Newcomen the newcomer." The governor chuckled at his own joke and went on. "He's been here only a few months. Spoke up just to hear his own voice, I think. Shouldn't even have been at the freemen's meeting. Then he and Billington got into it—arguing about some piece of land. Had nothing to do with the matter at hand." He wiped his chin on his sleeve. "Remember when that fool Morton held a feast up in Merrymount? Invited Indian women to come and mix with his men, and then led a pagan dance around a maypole!"

"God save us," John's stepmother said, nodding her head. "Did any speak for him?"

"Billington, of course. That drunken fool will stand against me no matter what the issue is."

"But when he isn't drunk—" That was a mistake. John had meant to keep quiet. He stopped himself, but not in time. His father wheeled around to face him.

"Were thou spoken to?"

"No, Father."

"Then be silent! Thou know nothing of it."

Behind his father's back, Young William rubbed his right index finger over his left in the shaming gesture. John's face flared in anger. He shook his fist at Will, but did so over to one side, where the others couldn't see it. Both boys knew better than to utter a sound.

"Did any others speak for Morton?" John's stepmother asked quickly.

"Allerton, the fool who brought Morton here in the first place. A disgrace! Allerton should know better. He's a disappointment himself. His trips to England to meet with the founders are supposed to lessen our debt, but he only makes it grow. Still they will elect him assistant, time after time."

"What did they decide to do about Morton?" his wife asked. She sat on a stool next to John and picked up her own bowl of beer.

"We're banning him from Plymouth—again—before he can do any more harm. Let Winthrop deal with him."

John's stepmother, John, and the Kempton children were cleaning up from supper when they heard shouting from outside.

"Bradford! Governor Bradford! Come out here, old

rascal! Will ye not come out to bid me farewell, sir?"
Everyone in the household rushed out the door.
Thomas Morton was shouting and struggling to keep
his footing in the muddy street as Captain Standish
and one of his men tried to pull him away. Many
people had already gathered, and others, hearing the
ruckus, were coming on the run.

Although many in the village wore brightly colored
clothing, Morton's outfit outshone them all. His large
hat was of violet felt with a long white feather that
draped down over the brim. His doublet was broadly
striped in shades of red, matching his darker red
breeches. Violet stockings and shiny black shoes
completed his outfit.

"Be still!" Captain Standish yelled as he cuffed
Morton on the back of his head, knocking off his hat.
"Ye had yer chance to speak!"

"Unhand me, Captain Shrimp!" Morton yelled. He
stooped to retrieve his hat, which he dusted off
against his leg.

Many in the crowd gasped at such blasphemy.
Miles Standish was indeed a short man. John had
even heard some people call Captain Standish "Captain Shrimp," behind his back. Known for his temper
as well as for his many skills, Miles Standish had an
important role in Plymouth. This was not a man to

be taken lightly. Morton was bold indeed to say such things to Standish's face.

Morton yanked his arm free of Standish's grip and straightened his clothing. "I bid ye fond farewell. I leave this place gladly," he said, addressing the crowd as well as the governor he now faced. "I want no more of yer silly little minds."

John Newcomen stepped between the governor and Morton. "Get ye gone! We don't need to listen to yer blather."

"Blather? Blather, ye say?" Morton shoved Newcomen, who fell backward into the mud.

Heads turned to the governor, who said nothing but kept his eyes on Morton.

Enjoying the crowd's reaction, Morton gave them more. He took a step closer to the governor.

"All the world treats this pitiful group and its laws with the same contempt as I. Ye call yerselves chosen people?" He turned with a sneer toward Newcomen, who stood now, his backside covered with mud. "There's a Chosen One all right."

Several in the crowd snickered.

Morton went on. "And chosen for what? This? This squalor?" He swept his arm around him with disgust. "Ye say I traded with the Indians? I did. They have as much right to guns as any. They hunt, and ye have often benefited by their hunting. Why shouldn't they have better tools to hunt with? The Good Lord knows they be better shots then the likes of these present. Ye say I conducted a pagan feast? The people of Merrymount are not pagans but God-fearing members of the Church of England. These are not crimes to any but such as yer pitiful selves. The accusations of murder in England are nonsense. 'Tis but an excuse to get rid of me." He glanced again at John Newcomen and then smiled broadly. "Pitiful indeed." Morton crossed his arms, waiting for reaction. It wasn't long in coming.

The mood of the crowd had changed from amusement to anger. There were first whispers then shouts: "He should be whipped!" "Put him in the stocks!" "Hog-tie him!"

Several of the men moved toward Morton, but John Billington stepped forward to stand beside Morton. "He has committed no crime. Let's be done with such foolishness and get on with the work."

Rachel said, "Good evening, Master Billington. I—"

Her mother's hand shot out and clapped firmly over the child's mouth. Quick as two shakes of a lamb's tail, Rachel was back in place, her face forcibly pressed against her mother's skirt.

John Bradford looked with sympathy at the Eaton

family. What an embarrassment Rachel was.

"Aye, ye'd do well to consider that work, John Billington." Master Eaton stepped out in front of his wife and daughter. "Let yer betters be concerned with this matter."

"I've as much right to speak as any in this village — more than many. I am a First Comer!" John Billington was as defiant as Thomas Morton. "There are others here who feel as I do." He looked around at the crowd, but no one spoke or came forward to join him.

Morton grinned and bowed to Billington. "I thank ye, kind friend," he said. "What say ye, Honorable Governor?" His voice was taunting, but Governor Bradford was not to be drawn into debate.

"The matter's been decided. Take him away," he said. He waved his hand in dismissal, stepped back into his house, and closed the door.

Miles Standish and two others grabbed Morton and dragged him away, nearly knocking over John Billington as they brushed by.

5

Dancing Spy

It was still mud season, and the footing was treacherous, but the air was sweet with spring. The sun shone brightly, and the few clouds in the sky were wisps of white. The willows near the brook had turned bright yellow, and there were the first tinges of light green on the branches of the trees. Most of the people of Plymouth found reason to be outside that late April morning, and many had shed their capes.

John Bradford was sharpening knives and axes on the grindstone up near the meetinghouse. The better drainage there made for dry ground, and he could keep the grindstone level. He'd begun with only the Bradford household's tools to sharpen, but other people saw what he was doing and decided to bring their own tools up.

"Might as well do these," one after another would say, adding more axes or knives to the pile. John grinned. He didn't mind. It was an easy task, and from his seat at the top of the hill, he could look down on the entire village.

His little sister Mercy was chasing after a lamb. She grabbed for it, but tripped and fell in the mud. Her cries brought John's stepmother out.

John Alden was fixing the thatch on his roof. His

wife, Priscilla, was standing below the ladder directing him. Several men were putting up a fence around the Whites' outer field. A group of women were boiling something in the large kettle. Chickens were scratching at whatever dry ground they could find.

John Bradford was grateful for his task for the day. There was no one to bother him; no one telling him what to do or how to do it. He began to whistle as he picked up the next knife.

Rachel came slipping and sliding up The Street, Spy bobbing on her shoulder as usual. The bird's wing had healed and the bandage was gone, but Master Billington had been right: it couldn't fly more than a foot or two. Rachel spotted John and headed toward him. John ceased his whistling and groaned, but there was no way to avoid her.

"Good morrow, John," she said cheerfully. "See what Sam made for me?" She held out a corn doll for his admiration.

John barely looked up. "Very nice," he said. "Go along, Rachel. I've work to do here."

He tested the knife-edge on a piece of straw. It was still not sharp enough, so he dipped water from the pail and dribbled some on the wheel. He tapped his foot on the treadle and placed the flat of the knife-edge against the wheel, setting off a squeal and a spray of sparks.

Rachel stooped beside John, holding the doll so that it touched the ground. Spy hopped off her shoulder and stood beside it. "Watch Spy dance with my dolly, John," she said.

Rachel began to sing and dance the doll around in the dirt:

We be three poor mariners;
Shall we go dance around, around;
Shall we go dance around.

Her voice was high and clear. Spy looked from the doll to Rachel and then began to caw in rhythm with the child's voice. With careful steps and an air of great dignity, the crow followed the doll around, turning as the doll turned.

John stopped the wheel and laughed in spite of himself. That foolish crow did appear to be dancing and singing.

Louder guffaws caused them both to look up. The governor and Rachel's father stood there, laughing as they brushed mud from their boots.

"A pretty song, child," the governor said when Rachel finished. "And a clever crow."

"Indeed it is," said her father. "That's a catchy tune, Rachel. I've not heard it before. How did thou come by it?"

"Master Billington taught it to me this very

morning," Rachel said, smiling up at the two men. "He knows lots of—"

Master Eaton grabbed his daughter roughly by the ear.

"Didn't I tell thee to stay away from that scoundrel!" he yelled as he dragged her down the hill.

Rachel cried out in pain and indignation. Spy ran after them, squawking loudly. The corn doll lay forgotten on the ground.

"Foolish child," the governor said, looking after them. He turned to John. "Say nothing!" he warned.

John put his head down as his father stomped up the stairs to the gun deck.

He finished the sharpening as quickly as possible and delivered the tools to each household. Then, before anyone could assign him another chore, he went down to his favorite rock by the sea. There, away from everyone and everything, he could think his own thoughts. Today as on many days, those thoughts were about his father.

6

Celebration

"That's not straight enough, John," Sam said. "And leave a bigger space before the next one. They can't bowl with them that way."

"'Tis just fine for bowling," John said as he stood up. "Thou can knock over more pins that way." He ran right into his friend, pushing Sam so hard that he fell and knocked over the pins.

"Oh, that's how 'tis going to be, is it?" Sam laughed as he got up. He brushed himself off and then dove for John's ankles. Soon the two were rolling over and over in the street, each trying to pin the other's shoulders to the dirt. Women, carrying dishes of food, stepped around them without comment. Moments later both boys were whistling as they walked arm in arm toward the food tables by the brook.

Everyone in the village seemed in a good mood that June afternoon. The sheepshearing was finished that morning, and a day of celebration had been declared. There were newcomers to welcome as well as the shearing to celebrate. The last of the Separatists who wanted to come from their congregation in Holland had arrived. It had been ten years since some of those old friends had seen each other—an occasion worthy of a celebration indeed.

Unfortunately, the new group had brought little other than themselves. It had been expected that they'd bring more provisions, perhaps more livestock for the village, and there was some grumbling among the non-Separatists that money had been spent to bring the new folks here when there was so much the colony still needed. But this had not been a hard winter. Most people were in a mood to celebrate.

The whole village had marched to the meeting-house at noontime for prayers. Now the fun could begin. Although some had harder, less agreeable tasks than others—cooking over the hot fires, for instance—there were smiles all around. The break from real work was too good to waste time grumbling. The only complaints were coming from the newly sheared sheep—bleating as they walked around looking slightly embarrassed.

Some children finished the job of pin-setting that John and Sam had begun and were now bowling.

Ed Doty struck up a tune on the pennywhistle, and some of the women, both John's and Samuel's step-mothers included, formed two lines and began to dance. Three other young men took up their own whistles and joined in. Others clapped to the rhythm.

Temporarily worn out from the wrestling, John and Sam each grabbed a chicken leg and plunked down, with their backs against a pine tree, where it was cool.

Kegs of beer had been tapped, and strong water was poured even before all the food was laid out. The talk and the laughter grew louder and more boisterous as the afternoon went on.

"Governor, will ye have beer or strong water?" someone called out.

"I'll have a bit of the strong," John's father answered, holding out his cup. "Not too much though. Got to be able to step right for the dancing. Take some up to the lads at the fort."

Ed Doty filled a pail with beer and headed up the hill.

"Hah!" Sam's father waved his cup about. "I recollect a time when yer step was anything but right."

"Do ye now," the governor said, raising an eyebrow. "And I suppose there's no stopping ye from telling about it, is there, Francis Eaton?"

John inched closer to listen. He loved to hear stories about his father.

"No sir, there is not," Master Eaton replied. He looked around at the group. "Not many here to remember it, and 'tis a tale that must not be forgotten," he said. "'Tis a side of the governor, so to speak, that few have seen." He laughed at the thought and took another sip of beer. "Right after the first landing on Cape Cod, it was. A group of us had come ashore to explore. Now this was our third trip to land. Remember it, Miles? Ye were there."

"Oh." Miles Standish's face lit up. "Oh, I know what yer talking of. Aye, I was right behind Bradford. Of course, he wasn't governor then. Carter was, but Will here fancied himself a leader even then."

John watched his father, who had an amused but wary look on his face, not quite sure where this story was going.

John Billington spoke up. "I was there," he said. "I was on that expedition."

Francis Eaton nodded. "So ye were, John, so ye were." He took another sip. "Anyway. Bradford leads the way though he knows no more than the rest of us about where we are or what's to come. We're wary of the Indians as we've seen none up close as yet, and so we're careful like."

He paused as some in the crowd added comments. "Aye, it was a fearful time." "Some arrows had been shot at them early on." "Narragansetts those were."

"So we're walking slow and single file and keeping a sharp eye out," Samuel's father continued. "Then Bradford spies a rope dangling from a pine near the beach. 'Look here!' he says. And we all march over."

"Ah!" Governor Bradford said. "'Tis the rope story, is it?" He laughed and took another sip of his drink.

"Must I stop?" Sam's father asked, although everyone knew he would not stop until the tale was told. "Shall I go no further, Will?"

John's father chuckled. "No. Go ahead, Francis, tell yer tale."

"With yer kind permission, then," Master Eaton said, bowing slightly to the governor. "'Tis Indian rope,' says our leader here." Sam's father nodded toward his friend and spoke with mock seriousness. "He's an expert, ye see. 'Notice how carefully they've made it. A clever snare for deer, it is,' says old Will. And he scuffs his right foot through the grass to uncover the hidden noose."

Several in the crowd were laughing now, knowing the tale. Others grinned in anticipation.

"And quick as a wink, he gives a yell, and there he is!" Francis Eaton shouted and motioned high in the air with his left hand. "Yelling, and dangling from one foot, six feet off the ground!"

Miles Standish guffawed and took up the story. "His free leg's waving about. His hat in the dirt, his cloak down about his face. And he's hollering, 'Get me down! Get me down!' As Francis said, 'twas a side of the man we hadn't yet seen, and are not likely to see again soon."

John laughed with the others at the thought of his dignified father in such a position.

"I thought to leave ye there," Francis Eaton shouted over the crowd's laughter. He clapped his friend on the back. "As a gift to the natives, but they made me cut ye down."

"And ye did it none too gently as I recall," said Governor Bradford. He bowed to the crowd, accepting their applause and laughter. "Well," he said. "I thought it best to show them how it worked." He put his cup down on the table. "Come, Francis. Let's see if yer feet are as lively as yer tongue."

"Now I'll tell ye a tale," John Billington said. He stepped forward to pour himself another cup, then turned and scowled as the crowd followed the governor out to the street.

"See what Spy can do now, Master Billington?" Rachel said softly as she stepped to his side.

"Get ye gone, child," he said. "I've no time for nonsense." He walked away up the hill.

Rachel bit at her lower lip, and her eyes brimmed with tears as she watched him leave.

Sam called out to her. "Come here, Rachel," he said. "Show us thy trick."

Rachel turned and smiled at Sam, but her attention quickly switched to the governor, who began to sing in a fine baritone: *One misty, moisty morning, when cloudy was the weather*. He led his line of men toward the line across the way as others picked up the song: *I chanced to meet an old man, a-clothed all in leather* . . .

It was evening. Several of the younger children were fast asleep in their mothers' arms, but still the crowd lingered, unwilling to put an end to such a good day.

"Tell us about the time the Narragansetts came, Governor," one of the young men said. Too full of food to eat another bite, Sam and John walked over to listen.

"Well, it was—"

A cry rang out from the fort: "Fire! Fire! Howland's!"

Children were dumped unceremoniously from laps. Everyone ran to the street and then to fetch buckets of water. John and Sam each grabbed a kettle, dumped out the contents, and dashed to the brook. Once full of water, however, the kettles were so heavy that it took both boys to carry one. As they hurried up the hill with the first kettle, they hollered to two of the Brewster servants to fill and bring up the other one.

Master Howland was up on the ladder, taking each container of water as it came and dumping it on the flames nearest the roof. Another man had the thatch hook and was pulling down thatch before it could catch fire.

If the flames reached the roof, the house was done for. Some people threw water on the outbuildings and the next house. A fire like this could sweep through the village in no time.

Elizabeth Howland and some of the other women and children carried clothing and furniture out of the house, setting things down on the street far from the blaze.

Fortunately, much of the area was still damp from last week's rains, and they were able to put out the fire before too much damage had been done.

"God was with us this time," John Howland said, and the crowd gathered at the front of the house for prayers of thanks.

John Bradford helped move the Howland things back into the house, then went with others to inspect the damage. The clapboards on about three feet of the back and two feet on the north side of the house were burned through to the wattle and daub from the ground almost to the roof. Other boards near it were scorched.

"We can fix this. The damage is slight," said one of the men.

"What started it, do ye think?" John Howland asked. "The fire in the hearth was low. All the cooking fires were far from here. Nothing should have caused a spark."

"It started outside the house, not in. There's deviltry afoot," Miles Standish said. "Or witchcraft. Was the house protected against witches?"

"Aye," John Howland said. "But that torch doesn't look like witches' doings to me." An empty bucket in each hand, he motioned with his foot toward a thick branch lying in the dirt a few feet from the house. It was charred on one end and had obviously been used as a torch.

"That couldn't have started the clapboards burning," Governor Bradford said. "They wouldn't catch unless a torch was held there a long time. Someone would have seen that happening."

"I'd a pile of kindling there beside the house," John Howland said. "'Twas sheltered and dry. The torch would get kindling burning soon enough, and that would catch the clapboards, but it wouldn't happen by accident. Who did this? Who tried to burn down my house?" He looked around at the crowd with suspicion. "Let the coward step forward!"

"Where's Billington?" Governor Bradford asked. "Has anyone seen Billington?"

John Bradford rolled his eyes. His father was at it again, blaming Billington first for everything that went wrong.

Several people shook their heads and looked around.

"Not since midafternoon," Francis Eaton said. "Why didn't he come to help when the alarm came?"

"Do ye think he started the fire? Would he do such a thing?" John Alden said. "It might have destroyed the whole village. Why would he do it?"

"Probably drunk again," said Francis Eaton.

"Drunk or sober, I put nothing past that man," Governor Bradford said.

John knew he should keep silent, but it all seemed so unfair. They were blaming the man with no proof whatsoever.

He said, "He didn't seem—"

His father whirled around, his dark eyes narrow with anger. "Home!" he said. He pointed up The Street. "Get thee home."

John knew better than to protest. He turned away, but before he could take a step, one of the new-comer's wives brushed past him, holding her two young sons by the scruffs of their necks.

"Tell them," she said as they got to the fire scene. "Tell them what thou did, for the sake of thy immortal souls."

Both boys were crying loudly.

"We didn't mean to," bawled the smaller of the two.

"We were looking for night crawlers and . . . Josiah set down the torch and . . ."

John hid his smile as he walked home.

7

Drunk

"Say it right. My name is Rachel. Say 'Rachel.'"

The boys had been walking down by the shore, enjoying the few moments of freedom after the long Sunday morning church service and noonday meal, when they heard Rachel's voice coming from the other side of a large rock.

Sam looked at John and grinned. "She's bound and determined to get that bird to talk."

"Give her credit for patience," John said.

They sat down on a piece of driftwood, idly watching sandpipers as they turned and ran in unison, searching the shallows of each wave as it swept the sand. Although much of the coast was rocky, there were sheltered coves like this one where the sand sloped gradually to the water. Here the waves broke farther out and then swept softly onto the shore.

"Thou should have been in church," they heard Rachel say.

John rolled his eyes. He could just imagine the reaction if that crow came into the church service.

"Get me more beer!"

With a quick startled glance at each other, both boys jumped up and ran around to the other side of the rock. Master Billington was propped up against a log. He held an upside-down tankard toward Rachel, who sat opposite him on the sand. Spy was beside her, pecking at a clamshell.

Rachel smiled at the boys. "Here's Sam and John," she said. "Maybe they can get thee some beer."

"Ah, two likely lads," Master Billington said. The front of his doublet was wet with spilled beer.

"Come away, Rachel," Sam said. He reached his hand out toward his sister. "Let's leave Master Billington alone."

Rachel whispered, "I think there's something wrong with him. He's talking funny."

Master Billington squinted as he looked up at John. "Yer Bradford's boy," he said. He shook his head in sympathy. "Poor sod."

Billington tossed the tankard into the sand and struggled to get up, but his feet slipped out from under him. He laughed as he fell back. "Give us a hand here," he said, stretching one hand out toward John.

John started to take the man's hand and then drew back. He was so used to doing whatever an adult told him to do that it was hard to disobey any command, but he thought it better for Master Billington to stay where he was.

"I'll help thee, Master Billington," Rachel said. She took his arm with both hands and tried to raise him.

"He's hurt, I think," she said. "Help him, Sam."

"He's not hurt, Rachel," Sam said with disgust. "He's drunk."

The man's good humor vanished instantly, and an angry expression spread over his face.

"Drunk, am I?" he shouted. "Drunk, ye say! I'll teach ye to disre . . . to disre . . ." He fell back against the log as the energy seemed to leave his body. "Aw, to hell with ye."

He picked up the tankard and put it to his lips. "Phaw!" he said, spitting out sand. He focused again on John.

"Yer father hates me." He giggled. "That's all right. What care I? I'm not overly fond of him. Governor Blah, I calls him."

Again his expression changed, this time to one of sadness. "They all hate me. Poor John Billington." Tears rolled down his face. He wiped them with the back of his sleeve.

John opened his mouth to speak but thought the better of it. There was no point in arguing with a drunk.

"Rachel," Sam said. "We have to go back to church. The afternoon session's about to start. We mustn't be late."

Rachel looked from Sam to Billington. "But we can't leave him here, Sam. He's crying."

"Aye," he said, taking her hand and pulling her away. "Aye, we can leave him. We must." Spy flew up to Rachel's shoulder, making a throaty sound.

John Billington paid no attention to the children. He muttered as if to some unseen person, sounding almost like Spy, as they left.

"Thou should have helped him," Rachel said reproachfully as they approached the meetinghouse. "He helped Spy when she was hurt."

"There's nothing we can do," Sam said. "He's had too much to drink."

"Was he very thirsty then?" she asked.

"I guess so," Sam said, winking at John.

"He's better off where he is," John said. "He's already in trouble for not being at church. If people see him drunk, especially on the Sabbath, they'll put him in the stocks again. They may put him there anyway."

"Why does thy father not like Master Billington?" Rachel said as they reached the meetinghouse. "My father doesn't like him either. The Bible says 'Love thy neighbor.' Master Billington is our neighbor, isn't he? Shouldn't they love him?" Spy hopped up on a bench and pecked at some crumbs.

"Shush now. 'Tis time for church," Sam said as he opened the door, grateful that there was no time to answer questions.

8

Rachel

A few days later John awoke at first light to find that the heat was already unbearable. He was not looking forward to the brush clearing that was his chore for the morning.

As he walked by the Eaton house, Sam stepped out of the door. "There's something wrong with Rachel," he said.

"Fever?" John asked.

Sam closed the door behind him and stood leaning against it. "No, no fever. 'Tis not like a sickness but . . . She's not moving, John. She stares straight ahead like a . . . like a . . ." He gave it up and went back to his original statement. "Something's wrong. She won't talk. And she looks . . ." He groped for words. "Different."

"That must be a relief—having her quiet for a change," John said. "She's just having fun with thee, Sam. That one's always up to something. Come help me clear brush. We can work better without her jabbering."

"'Tis not like that, John. She's not moving, and she hasn't said a word since late yesterday. She won't eat."

"'Tis the heat," John said. "Nobody can eat much in this heat.

"'Tis more than that," Sam insisted. "She won't play—not even with Spy. Something's wrong, John. Come see."

"No, I—"

Ignoring John's protests, Sam pulled him inside. He pushed him through the front room where several of the other people in the Eaton household stood talking quietly. Sam then led John into the room where Goodwife and Master Eaton sat beside their daughter on a bench. Her parents looked up as John and Sam entered, but Rachel's usually animated face gave no sign of recognition.

"Good morrow, Mistress Eaton, Master Eaton," John said, shifting from one foot to the other in the doorway.

"Look, Rachel," her mother said. "John's come to see thee. Thou like John. Say good morning to him."

"Good morrow, Rachel," John said, stepping forward with a jerk as Sam pushed him from behind. He barely avoided stepping on Spy, who was sitting quietly on the floor close to Rachel's feet.

There was no reaction. Sam bent to pick up Spy. He placed the bird on his sister's shoulder, where it pecked gently at her cheek. She gave no sign that she felt it.

"Have thou taught Spy any new tricks?" John asked.

It was like talking to a stump. There was no response; no change in her face.

Without another word, John left the house and went directly to the Fuller house. There he knocked loudly on the door.

Goodwife Fuller opened it. One look at his face told her that this was not a social call. "What is it, John?"

"Rachel," he said.

"She's been hurt?"

"No. Aye. I don't know." John tried to find a way to explain what he'd just witnessed. "Something terrible has happened. She won't move. She doesn't talk."

"Well, perhaps she's—"

John didn't let her go on. "Come!" He grabbed her hand and dragged her along the street.

"What? John! Stop! Wait!"

John paid her no mind. At the Eaton house, he pushed her in before him. "Do something!" he ordered.

The whole Eaton family was just as he had left them, but now Goodwife and Master Eaton looked more hopeful, as the woman who knew so much about sickness and the herbs that could cure it entered the room. They moved to the side to give her access to their daughter.

"Thank thee, John," Sam murmured.

Goodwife Fuller knelt beside Rachel. "Good morrow, Rachel," she said. "Having a bit of trouble?" She felt of the child's forehead, pulled each eyelid down and looked into her eyes. Rachel offered no resistance as Goodwife Fuller pulled back the sleeves of Rachel's garment and examined her arms.

"Let me have a few minutes with Rachel, please," she requested. They all left the room.

Master Eaton leaned against the side of the house as his wife paced back and forth, wringing her hands on her apron. The others in the household stood near John and Sam over to the side, their heads bowed in prayer. They could hear Goodwife Fuller's soft voice occasionally.

In a few minutes Goodwife Fuller came out. "When did this start?" she asked.

"She was fine at noon," Rachel's mother offered. "Ate her dinner just like always. Chattered nonstop. Gave too much of it to Spy. I scolded her. Not too much," she hastened to add. "Anyway, she paid me no mind." Goodwife Eaton shook her head. "Then off she went to the woods."

"I scolded her too," her father said. "Perhaps I was too harsh, but she spends too much time with that bird. Neglects her work and her lessons. She must learn to read and write."

He looked at the others for approval. Getting no reaction, he went on. "When she didn't come back for supper, we all went out to look for her."

"I found her at the edge of the woods," Sam said. "Just sitting there against the tree. She was so still I wouldn't have even noticed her but for Spy. I ran to get Father."

Master Eaton nodded. "That bird was cawing and hopping around, but Rachel . . . she was . . . like this," he finished lamely. "I picked her up and carried her here." His voice choked. "I thought she was being willful. I shook her. Threatened to whip her."

"There she's sat ever since," his wife said. "If she slept at all, it was sitting up when I dropped off." A fearful look came over her face. "Is it a witch do ye think? Has some witch cast her spell over my poor child?"

"Did ye hang the broken jar in the chimney?" asked Mistress Fuller.

"We did," Master Eaton said. "And we buried the jar of pins under the hearth."

"I put the red felt at the top of both windows myself," Sam added.

Goodwife Fuller nodded. "There should be no witch here then," she said. "Pray for her. Whatever is wrong with the child, 'tis something no herbs can remedy. I'll send my husband over this evening. He's off hunting with the others now. Make her as comfortable as ye can and keep watch and keep praying."

9

Missed Chances

"Where art thou going, Sam?"

John had hurried to the Eaton house first thing in the morning. He'd been about to knock when the door swung open, and Sam emerged.

"To the Billingtons'. Come with me." Sam spoke over his shoulder as he strode down the street. John fell into step beside him.

"The Billingtons'? Why?"

"Because she just sits there, John. It's as if her body is still there, but her soul is gone. Mother cried all night. No one slept."

"And thou thinks the Billingtons can help?" John couldn't believe what he was hearing.

"Not all of them, just Master Billington."

"How can he help?"

"I don't know, but Rachel loves him. No one else seems to be able to help. Maybe he can."

Master Billington was fixing the fence at the side of his house. He looked up as the boys approached.

"Good morrow, Master Billington," Sam said.

Master Billington nodded. "What do ye want?"

"I want ye to come to our house," Sam said.

"Oh, ye do, do ye? Inviting me for supper, perhaps? Wait! I'll tell me wife to put on her fancy clothes."

He waved them away and turned back to his digging.

"Be gone with ye. I want none of yer foolishness."

"Please, Master Billington," Sam said. "'Tis my sister Rachel. Ye helped her with her crow, remember?"

"Of course I remember. Do ye think I'm daft?" Master Billington said suspiciously. "What of it?"

"Well, now there's something wrong with Rachel."

"Wrong with her?"

"Aye," Sam said. "She won't talk, and she just sits and stares. 'Tis like she's been bewitched or something."

"And what do ye expect me to do about it?"

"I don't know," Sam said. "If ye just come and see her. Maybe ye can think of something—say something."

Master Billington spoke over his shoulder as he went on fixing the fence. "Get the Fullers, then, if she's sick. I'm no doctor, and I've got no magic words for the lass."

"Come on, Sam." John spoke for the first time. "There's no help for Rachel here."

"Yer right about that," Master Billington yelled after them as they walked back to Sam's house.

Sam's shoulders were slumped as they neared the Eaton house. He turned toward his friend. "Will no one help?"

John glanced back over his shoulder and then

turned and pointed down the road. "Look," he said. Hammer in hand, Master Billington was coming up The Highway.

"Where is she?"

"In here, Master Billington." Sam opened the door and was about to step inside when his father appeared in the doorway.

"Come in, Sam," his father said and then looked over to see John Billington's approach. "What do ye want, Billington?"

Master Billington stopped. "The boy asked me to come," he said.

"Get ye gone," Sam's father said. "We've troubles enough here without the likes of ye." He pulled Sam inside and slammed the door.

John hung his head. By the time he could bring himself to look toward Master Billington, the man was already halfway down the street.

John was at the brook, scrubbing out the family's big kettle with sand, when he felt a hand on his shoulder. He looked up, thinking it was Sam, and then jumped up when he realized it was his father.

The governor grinned. "Go on with thy work, John."

John was wary. "Am I doing it wrong?"

His father shrugged. "I don't know. Art thou?"

"I hope not, Father." John went back to his scrubbing but kept looking up at his father. It made John nervous to have him there. He waited for the criticism he was sure would come.

"Do thou mind sharing thy peaceful spot?" his father asked.

"Er, no, Father."

The governor took off his shoes and stockings. He sighed contentedly as he lowered his feet into the water. "Ahhhhh," he said, wiggling his toes beneath the surface. "Feels good. 'Twas a long meeting."

For a few minutes there was only the sound of sand scratching in the pot as John scrubbed.

"Is Rachel still ailing?" His father lifted his feet from the water and placed them on a rock. Water trickled down on all sides.

"Aye, Father."

"Have thou seen her this morning?"

"No, Father."

"Why not?"

"I . . . we . . ." He started to explain and then thought the better of it. He certainly couldn't tell his father he'd gone with Sam to try to get John Billington's help. Neither could he lie to his father and make up some story about trying to help in another way. His father would hear what had happened soon enough.

"Nothing seems to help," John said finally. "There must be something I can do, but I can't think what. Seems like we've tried everything."

"It may be the Devil's work," his father cautioned. "Prayer is the answer. 'Tis in God's hands."

John turned toward his father. "Tell me, Father. Tell me what I can do, and I'll do it."

His father raised his eyebrow and had a slight smile on his face as he looked over at his son.

"I did tell thee, John. Pray. Don't be prideful, son. If it were God's will, we would know what else to do for the child. 'Tisn't, and so we do not."

John's face reddened. He'd said the wrong thing again. He put his head down and concentrated on the scrubbing. He sighed, realizing that this was just one of the many household pots left to scrub that morning. Thankfully one of the Kempton girls had the chamber pots to clean. That was a terrible chore, and there were three of them. Thinking about the crowded conditions in the household reminded John about his lean-to idea.

"Father," he said. "Our house is small."

"Have thou just noticed that?" his father said, smiling.

"No," John said. "But with the Kemptons and the others, 'tis so crowded. If we had a little more space, we'd all be more comfortable."

His father's manner changed abruptly to a stern one. "Comfort? Comfort is your goal?" he asked. "Comfort is not for the Chosen. We work for the common good. We share what we have with those who need it. What bounty we have to spare is sent to the founders that our colony may someday be free and clear of debt. We don't use the time or the money for things we do not need—like more room in a house that is more than adequate."

John put his face down quickly. "Aye, Father," he said.

"Keep your thoughts to prayer for Rachel and for God's grace. Let comfort go."

Again there was no sound but the babble of the brook and the cry of a catbird. John kept his eyes to his work and didn't see his father's hand reach out toward his son's shoulder, hesitate, and then retreat.

His father put on his stockings and shoes and stood. "Let us pray for Rachel, John," he said. John stood beside his father, head bowed.

10

Missing

"Any change?" John asked Sam the next morning as they headed out to get the hay in from a field about a quarter of a mile west of the village. At least the heat had lifted, and there was a breeze this morning.

Sam's expression was grim. "Not much," he said. "She moves about a bit now. We got her to sip some milk last night, and she ate a bit of porridge this morning, but she won't talk. Doesn't seem to care about anything. Elder Brewster and Reverend Smith led us in prayers most of the night."

"What did Master Fuller say?"

"Not much. He bled her, but—"

"At least she's eating. Give her time. She'll come round," John said.

"Perhaps," said Sam. "God will not let her die, will he, John? She's so good . . . so . . ."

John clapped his hand on his friend's shoulder. "Go back home, Sam," he said. "Thou shouldn't try to work today."

"No," Sam replied. "'Tis better to work. There's nothing to do at home." His voice choked, and he swallowed hard. "She just sits there."

With no further conversation, the boys picked up

rakes from the barn and went out to the field, where the work was already under way. The hay had been cut several days ago. Now that it had dried, it must be taken into the barns.

Since the division of cattle three years before, each household was responsible for the care of their own livestock and whatever it produced, but they all worked together getting in the hay and feed, taking it as needed from central storage.

Haying was hard work, and the boys worked up a sweat in no time. Halfway through the morning, John looked up to see Sam's mother standing with Rachel under the ash tree at the edge of the field. As usual Spy was on Rachel's shoulder. John nudged Sam, and they walked over.

Goodwife Eaton handed a jug of water to Sam and then pushed her daughter forward. Sam eagerly put the jug to his lips and drank before handing it to John.

"Here, Rachel," Sam's mother said. "Give John and Samuel some cornbread."

With no emotion on her face, Rachel held out the plate, and John and Sam each took a piece.

"Thank thee, Rachel," Sam said in a loud, falsely cheerful voice.

Spy hopped down onto the plate, knocking it to the ground. Rachel didn't react. She held her hands out as if still holding the plate. John reached down, picked it up, and handed it to Sam's mother, keeping his worried eyes on Rachel all the while.

With a resigned sigh, Goodwife Eaton took the plate in one hand, turned her daughter by the shoulder with the other, and led her away. After a few pecks at the crumbs, Spy squawked and ran after them.

Desperate for anything that might help Rachel, John broke a twig off the tree.

"Here, Sam," he said. "Put this under Rachel's pillow tonight when she's asleep."

"Under her pillow? Why?"

"'Tis ash. Witches fear it. People in Holland used it often. If 'tis a witch's spell she's under, it may help."

"That's pagan," Sam protested, drawing back his hand.

"'Tis but a tiny twig. No one will know."

"What if 'tis a sin, John?"

"But what if it helps?"

"Aye," Sam said. "What if it helps." He put the twig in his pocket. There were tears in his eyes as the boys headed back into the field.

"And keep praying," John said. He was a bit nervous about offering such a pagan cure although he knew many in the community used such devices to ward off witches and their spells. "She's getting better. She's walking around now. 'Tis a big improvement. Be patient, Sam. The Bible says 'Those who wait on the Lord shall inherit the earth.'" Quoting the Bible made John feel less guilty.

He looked out to sea. The wind had been coming from the northeast. Now it had shifted to an east wind bringing dampness from the ocean. A fog was drifting in. "Weather's changing. We'd best hurry."

Everyone hustled to get the hay inside the barn before dampness descended. Aching and tired, the boys headed for home when the job was finished. By that time, the fog was quite thick. The boys could hear voices but they were well along The Street before they could see a crowd in front of John's house.

"What's going on?" John wondered aloud. Sam shrugged and turned to his own house.

"I'll see to Rachel," he said, "and find a way to use this." He took the twig from his pocket and held it up.

"She'll get better, Sam," John called out to him. "She has to. Tomorrow will be better."

Sam's head was down as he put the twig back in his pocket and entered his house.

John's father was in the center of a group of men, but he looked up and nodded at John's approach.

"How long has he been gone?" asked one man.

"Hard to say," said another. "A week, maybe."

"No, not a week," said the first. "I saw him Monday, I think."

"'Tis hard to say how long he's been gone," Elder Brewster said. "Apparently, he's apt to go off by himself. He had his fishing pole and his fowling piece. He lives with the Aldens, and they weren't alarmed until this morning."

"Who is it?" John whispered to Ed Doty. "Who is missing?"

"John Newcomen."

To John's surprise, his father turned and addressed him directly. "John, we're organizing a search for Newcomen although I don't know how far we'll get. If the fog gets any thicker, we'll have to call it off. Go and tell thy mother that I need thee for the search."

John nodded, trying not to show how pleased he was. He opened the door and yelled, "I'm going with Father!" and then quickly rejoined the men.

It wasn't all that uncommon for someone to become lost, and such search parties had to be formed. Much of the land along the coast had been cleared long before they had come to Plymouth. To the west lay the wild lands, thick growths of endless woods where few of the settlers dared to go. Still, people did wander off sometimes, and there were dangers: rivers, cliffs, and ravines, wild beasts, of course, and there were the Indians. The local Indians were friendly, but there was always the chance that things could go wrong, especially with someone like Newcomen, who wouldn't have been used to dealing with them.

The men were organizing in groups of five for the search. The governor motioned John over to where his group of four, including Master Fuller and two servants, were waiting. John tried not to show his further satisfaction. His father wanted John in his own group.

"Now mind ye stay in sight of the man to yer left and the one to the right," Governor Bradford said, still addressing the crowd. "What we don't need is anyone else getting lost. In this fog that will be all too easy. Every man should carry something white or brightly colored in the left hand. Does each group have at least one light? It won't shine far in this fog, but 'twill make it easier to keep each other in sight." He looked around and nodded as torches were held up. "When night falls, turn back unless the fog has lifted. Fire two shots if ye find him. All right then. Careful now. God guide our footsteps."

John took out his white handkerchief and held it in his left hand. He squared his shoulders and stepped off as his group headed toward the woods. His father was on his left, Master Fuller on the right. The other groups disappeared into the fog almost immediately.

The fog changed the woods completely. The trees and vines assumed ghostly shapes. Sounds were muffled and seemed to come from all directions at once. They could hear the voices of the other groups and occasional calls. "John! John Newcomen!"

There was no path and the underbrush was in full growth. Branches and briars pulled at their clothing and further slowed the search.

John walked slowly at first, looking down and then to the left and right with every step. His father was stepping ahead slowly.

As they walked on through the fog, John's thoughts turned to Rachel and then to the ash twig. It was against the teachings to use such charms, but many did. He hoped he hadn't offended God. Still, he felt that they had to try everything possible.

John quickened his step as the underbrush grew less dense around his feet, pulling slightly ahead of his father, pushing forcefully through the bushes. He kept his head down. He didn't want to stumble. Wouldn't it be wonderful if he was the one to find Newcomen? Perhaps the man was wounded, maybe with a broken leg. John would help him to his feet. "Father," he would say proudly, "here he—"

The last thing John remembered was the glimpse of a large tree directly ahead of him. He was moving too quickly to stop and hit it face on, full force.

The next thing John heard was the sound of his step-mother's voice: "He's coming to." What was she doing in the woods? John opened his eyes. His step-mother was holding a cold rag to his head, which hurt terribly.

"Mother?" he said.

"How do thou feel?"

He was in his parents' bed. John struggled to sit up, but that made him dizzy. He fell back against a pillow.

"What happened?" he asked. "How did I get here?"

"Thou fell." His father's voice thundered from across the room, where he stood with some of the Kempton family. His angry voice made John's head throb even more. Moving his eyes without turning his head, John could see his father filling his cup from a pitcher and, without another word, leaving the room.

John looked at his stepmother for an explanation as the Kempton family followed his father out of the room.

"Thou hit thy head on a rock," she said. "Thy father and John Alden carried thee home."

"Did they find Newcomen?"

He tried not to think of the shame of it. What had his father said to the others? What had he said to his wife? Everyone must be talking about it. John could just imagine how much chatter there would be. In this house and in every house in the village, people must be saying, "The governor's son failed again. Not much like his father, is he? Such a disappointment."

His stepmother shook her head. "The search was called off."

"Because of me?"

"They couldn't have gone on much longer anyway," she said. "The fog was too thick. They'll go out again in the morning." She stood. "Just rest, John. There's quite an egg on thy head." She went into the other room, leaving John alone with his aching head and his shame.

11

Searching

It seemed to John that he was awake all night, listening to the snores of the others in the bed, but he must have slept eventually, for when he opened his eyes, it was morning. His sister Mercy was standing beside the bed.

"Good," she said. "I thought thou were dead." She turned and yelled, "Mother! John's awake! He's not dead."

"Hush, child. Of course he's not dead." John's stepmother hurried into the room as John sat up. "Good morrow, John," she said. "Feeling better?"

"Some," he said, gingerly touching the bump on his head. At least the dizziness was gone. "Father?" he asked, looking around.

"Searching," she said. "The fog's lifted." She went out to the hearth, ladled some porridge into a bowl, and brought it in to John.

"No," he said, turning away. "I'm not hungry."

"Thou need food," she said. Her tone was matter-of-fact, neither pleading nor commanding. John took the bowl. "Mercy, go play with Will. Leave John alone," she said.

Mercy left the room, and John's stepmother filled her cup. She pulled a stool up nearer John.

"What did Father say about me?" John asked.

"Not much," she said. "His mind was on the search."

"He blames me, doesn't he?" John said.

"It was an accident, John. No one blames thee. He thanks God as we all do that thou weren't more seriously hurt."

"I've disappointed him," John said. "He must be sorry I ever came."

"Came? Came to Plymouth?"

"Aye."

"No, he's not sorry. What about thee, John? Art thou sorry?" She dipped a cloth in water and placed it gently on his forehead.

He winced at the touch. "Sorry I came?"

She nodded.

"No. 'Tis better than Holland, mostly. Sam's a good friend. And thou."

His stepmother smiled as she added, "And Young Will, and Mercy."

Truthfully, John seldom thought much about his half brother and sister. They were just two more bodies in the already crowded household. Young Will was a pest sometimes, and Mercy was too young to bother with. "'Tis good here. Mostly," he went on. "But with Father . . ." He tried shaking his head, but it hurt too much. "I try. But 'tis so hard."

His stepmother nodded. "I know, John. He tries too. 'Tis hard on him as well."

John gave a slight nod. "Because I'm not . . . Because I can't . . ." He choked back a sob and drew in a breath. "I'll never be the son he wants."

"Thou art a fine young man, John. And much comfort to us both."

"Thou knew him when he was young." It was a statement, not a question.

His stepmother smiled. "I've known thy father— oh, from way back. We played together some when we were little back in England. And then, during the twelve years in Holland. It was a small community of Separatists. We all stayed together as much as we could."

"What was he like when he was a boy?"

"Oh, he was full of it, John. And often in trouble. A wild one. My father warned me against him."

"He was wild? My father?"

His stepmother grinned and nodded. "There were many who thought he'd never amount to much."

"What happened to make him so perfect, then?" John asked.

"Oh, no one is perfect, John. Thou mustn't think it."

"Well, nearly perfect, then," said John.

"His parents died before he was twelve," his stepmother said. "That changed him some. He lived with an uncle for a while, but they didn't get on well."

"Did he try hard to please his uncle?" John asked.

His stepmother shrugged. "I suppose so, for a while. Mostly he changed when he found the Separatist path to God. He joined Elder Brewster's church. His uncle was Church of England and didn't approve of the Separatists. Things got worse and, eventually, thy father moved in with Elder Brewster."

"He pleased Elder Brewster, then?" John asked.

His stepmother nodded. "Very much," she said. "Elder Brewster was like a father to him—still is. He's quite proud of the man thy father became. We all are."

"I'm always . . . To my father I . . ." Again he started to shake his head, but stopped when it hurt. "Perhaps Young William will turn out to be someone he's proud of."

"Thy father loves thee, John, as he does Young William. 'Tis just that thou art older, and he wants so much for thee. We both do."

Even talking about his father was hard, but he didn't want the conversation to end. There was such comfort with his stepmother.

"Tell me about when thou came to Plymouth. What was it like for thee?"

"Well, I was frightened, of course."

"Of my father?"

"Oh no, not of thy father." She shook her head. "Of coming to a new land. I was with my sister and her family but still I was frightened. Leaving all I knew behind in Holland. I'd done that before when I went to Holland from England. Now I was doing it again. I was frightened of the dangers here as well. So many had died." She took a deep breath. "I'd not heard from thy father after he came to Plymouth."

"Did thou know my mother?"

"All of us who settled in Holland knew each other," his stepmother said. "Thy mother was a fine woman, John. I thought a lot of her."

"I wish I could have known her," John said. He absently spooned some porridge into his mouth.

"Aye, but God did not will it so." She paused a moment before she went on with her story. "I knew when the group arrived here, of course. Thou know how we hungered for news of the Old Comers in Holland, but I never heard directly from thy father until the letter came."

"The letter. What did it say?"

"Well, many things, but mostly he asked me to come to America and be his wife." She smiled.

"And thou came."

"Indeed I did. On the very next ship."

"The *Anne*."

"Aye, on the *Anne*," she agreed.

"Was the voyage rough?"

"It was rough. Like thine, I suppose."

"Were thou sick?" John asked, remembering his own miserable days at sea.

"Oh, my! I was sick for days."

"And when thou landed here, did Father come to greet thee?" He kept his eyes directly on his step-mother's, trying to gauge whether or not she told the truth.

She nodded. "He did."

"And was he glad to see thee? Did he take thy hand? Did he hug thee? Kiss thee?"

She blushed. "No, no. He wouldn't have done such things."

"Then how did thou know he was glad?"

She smiled. "His eyes, John. His eyes were glad."

John thought about the look in his father's dark brown eyes when they turned his way. Had there been gladness in those eyes when John had arrived at Plymouth? Had he ever seen gladness in his father's eyes directed at him? John didn't think so. He ate some more porridge.

"Tell me about the wedding, Mother. Was it like the Whites'?"

"Oh, it was fine, John. It was fine." She smiled, her eyes sparkling. "Most weddings are times of celebration, but this was special. It was a big thing for the governor to be married. I was so proud. I wore bright blue. Thou know the skirt; I wear it still. And when I stepped out of the door, they were all lined up in the street.

"I walked up to where thy father stood waiting for me. And then Massasoit came in at the bottom of the hill. The great leader of the Wampanoags came to my wedding, John." Her eyes widened, remembering the sight. "That was something. He wore great long necklaces that hung down almost to the ground, and a beaver-fur robe. And he brought one of his wives, John, and she was all dressed in deerskin. And many, many of his men came. Oh, and they brought food— much food for the wedding feast, and gifts. Everybody stared because . . . Well, because it was really something to see. All those Indians in the village at once."

John nodded. It would have been a sight, all right. Not that Indians in Plymouth Village were so unusual. The natives came frequently, alone or in small groups. Indian women, sometimes with children clinging to their sides, came to sell small things. Hobbamuck, one of Massasoit's counselors, lived with his wives and children just outside the palisade on the south side of the brook. John had been scared of them at first, but no longer. Still, a whole group of

Indians coming at once for the governor's wedding—
John would like to have seen that.

"And Father?" he asked. "What did Father do?"

"He accepted the gifts they brought, and he
thanked them for coming. He was very pleased."

"And thou could tell he was pleased by looking at
his eyes."

"Well, he smiled too, John, and he said how
pleased he was. Of course he was pleased. It was a
great honor."

"And what did he say to thee, Mother?"

"He said I looked comely."

"That's all he said? That thou looked comely?"

His stepmother blushed again. "He said much
more, John."

"Out loud? Did he say nice things out loud?"

"Softly. One says such things softly, John."

"But he said them?"

"He said them."

John sighed and put down his bowl. He took the
cloth off his head and stood to test his legs. When
they didn't crumple beneath him, he walked slowly
to the door.

"He never has said nice things to me. Not even
softly," he said as he stepped outside, nearly bumping into his father, who was just coming in.

"John!" His father stepped back in surprise, and

John stumbled backward into the doorway.

"Father!" he said, struggling to keep his footing. "Father, I'm sorry."

"Aye," his father said grimly. "Sorry indeed."

John didn't bother to try to look at his father's eyes. He knew what he'd see there. The governor brushed by John and went into the house. John started to follow and then changed his mind. He headed for Sam's house. Even with the worry over Rachel, it was a better place to be right now.

12

Found

For the next three mornings John sat silently through breakfast, hoping against hope that his father would ask him to rejoin the search, but the governor talked to others in the household and then left each morning without a word or glance in John's direction.

Most of the men in the village were involved in the search as it intensified, so John and Sam took frequent sentry duty. At noon on the third day of their watch, Rachel came up to the gun deck by herself, carrying bowls of porridge for their dinner.

"Why, here's our Rachel," Sam said, surprised and pleased at this sign of her recovery.

"I'm glad to see thee, Rachel," John said, echoing Sam's cheerful tone. "What good things have thou brought us?"

Rachel turned her big blue eyes toward John, but the expression on her face was so sad that John almost wished for a return of the blank stare.

"Any news on the search?" John asked. It was a foolish question. There was no news. From their post, they'd have seen and heard any approach by members of the search parties. It was just that

Rachel's sad face made John uneasy. He felt he had to say something.

Rachel's eyes filled with tears. She gave a loud sob, turned, and rushed down the stairs and down the street toward home. Spy flapped her wings, trying to stay on her shoulder.

Both boys leaned over the rail to watch Rachel disappear into the Eaton house.

"I'm sorry," John said. "I didn't mean to upset her." He picked up their dinner bowls, which Rachel had dropped.

Sam shrugged and gave a slight smile. "At this point, 'tis good even to see tears. Who knows why she shed them? She is getting better. Still, the least little thing seems to upset her, and she will not talk."

It was almost dark when the boys heard shouts and saw the searchers coming back, Miles Standish in the lead. Behind him two men carried someone.

The whole group marched to the front of the meetinghouse and laid the body down. John and Sam leaned over the rail to watch as the others gathered round; women and children scurried up the hill from their houses to join them.

Sam's mother, holding Rachel by the hand, started up the hill, but Rachel screamed and fell down on the street, crying loudly. Her mother picked her up and carried her back into the house.

For a moment the crowd was distracted by Rachel, but soon turned its attention back to the body. Torches were lit and, from their perch, the boys could now see the body of John Newcomen.

"Indians!" declared one of the men.

Another shook his head. "Look at the wound, man. 'Tis a bullet that killed him, not an arrow."

"The Indians have guns, thanks to that fool Morton," John Howland said.

"Why would an Indian kill Newcomen?" Governor Bradford asked. "He's had no dealings with them, has he?"

Elder Brewster shook his head. "No, and we'd have heard if there'd been trouble." He paused. "Could it be that he took his own life?"

"Surely not," Francis Eaton said. "If he wanted to kill himself, why go so far into the woods?" He looked around at the others. "Was he upset? In trouble? Who knew him well?"

"He lived with us," Priscilla Alden said. "He was a very nice man—good to the children and a hard worker, wasn't he, John?"

John Alden nodded. "He kept to himself. He had no wife, no family here, although I think he had a sweetheart back home."

"He wouldn't have . . ." Priscilla swallowed hard. "Done this," she finished weakly.

"Could it have been an accident? Someone aiming at a deer, perhaps?" John Alden asked.

"A bullet through the chest is not a likely accident," Samuel Fuller said. "Besides, if it was an accident, the shooter would have owned up to it by now. No one can seek God's grace with a man's death on his soul. Even an accidental death."

"He could have shot himself by accident."

"Not in the chest," Samuel Fuller said firmly. "Not in the chest."

"Who would have meant him harm?" Priscilla Alden asked.

"Well, he was quarrelsome," John Howland said. "Morton quarreled with him."

"Aye," said John Alden. "I'd put little past that Morton. Pagan fool!"

Governor Bradford spoke. "Most of us quarreled with Morton, but 'tis a long way from a quarrel to a killing." He shook his head, looking down at the body and then around at the still-gathering crowd. "It could have been anyone. There are settlers all up and down the coast now. Someone we don't even know could have had grief with him."

"Who wasn't in the search party?" Priscilla Alden asked.

"Almost every man joined in the search at one time or another," her husband said. "That doesn't mean much. They could have murdered the man and still joined the search."

"Can ye say how long he's been dead?" Governor Bradford asked the surgeon.

"Hard to tell," Samuel Fuller said. "At least three days. Could have been more."

"He quarreled with Billington at the last freemen's meeting," Governor Bradford said. He looked around for John Billington and spotted him standing with his son Francis at the edge of the crowd. "Ye quarreled with him, didn't ye, Billington? Did ye quarrel again?"

John Bradford nudged Sam and whispered, "He'll blame Billington before this is over. Even this."

"No, no!" John Billington took a step backward, raising his hands as if to defend himself from attack. "It was nothing! We helped to find him. Ye cannot blame me for this." He turned and walked back to his house with his head down, his son at his side.

Governor Bradford watched them walk back down the street. John thought his father's face betrayed his suspicions.

"Newcomen quarreled with Allerton, didn't he?" John Alden asked. "Where's Allerton? He wasn't in the search."

"He's gone up to Massachusetts Bay for trading," Governor Bradford said. "Been gone a week or more.

Wasn't Allerton, but it could have been any of those folks up there." He looked around. "'Tis dark and time we all were inside."

Many people, suddenly aware of the darkness, turned to hustle back into their houses.

"Pray for his soul. We'll form a plan tomorrow," the governor called after them. He drew a deep breath and spoke to the men who had carried the body. "For now, take him into the meetinghouse. The women can get him ready for burial, as there's no family to do it. We'll commit him to God's care tomorrow."

13

The Books

"She cries most of the time," Sam said a few mornings later as he and John headed out to the far gardens, each to work on his own family's plot. "'Tis terrible. I never thought I'd miss the silence." He shook his head as if to clear it, and then asked, with some embarrassment, "Do thou know of another charm, John?"

John was equally embarrassed. "I don't. Has she said anything?"

Sam shook his head. "Not really, but I think she whispers to Spy sometimes."

"A good sign," John commented. "At least thou know she can talk."

Sam nodded. They walked on together.

"Who do thou think killed Master Newcomen?" Sam asked, anxious to think about something besides his sister.

John shrugged. "I expect 'tis someone outside of Plymouth—probably up in Massachusetts Bay."

"Could it have been Morton, do thou think?"

John nodded. "I don't know. He hates the colony. Maybe he'd do something to bring us grief."

"Nothing like suspicion to get folks going at each

other," Sam said. "Does thy father really think 'tis Master Billington?"

"I don't know. He doesn't come out and say so, but every time he talks about the murder, he mentions Billington's name. I'm afraid he'll find a way to put it on him."

"Surely not," Sam said. "Thy father is a just man, John. He'll do the right thing."

"Aye," John said. "The right thing."

His father hardly seemed aware of the food John's stepmother set before him that evening. His whole body sagged against the table, and for the first time, as John looked at his father's face, he thought about how old the man was. Forty, as John figured it. Not as old as many in the colony, but tonight his father looked like an old man.

The governor sipped at his beer. "We've sent men up to Massachusetts Bay to tell Allerton about the murder and to ask questions there."

"Thou thinks the one who did it is one of the Bay Colony then?" his stepmother asked. "Could it be Morton?"

The governor cocked his head. "'Tis possible," he said. "I hope it is Morton or someone like him. I can't bear to think it was done by one of ours. A murderer in Plymouth Colony." He shook his head.

"We're the Chosen Ones—brothers and sisters working together to do God's will. If the murderer is one of ours, it will be as bad as Cain killing Abel. It cannot be. It must not be. We've worked so hard—come so far. There have been arguments, disagreements, many of them over the years. Just men may differ, but to take arms against another soul in Plymouth? It must not be."

"Can thou find out?" she asked.

"I don't know. I don't know," the governor said, rubbing his forehead. "No one saw it. No one seems to have had reason to kill the man. Several appear to have disliked him, Billington among them, but not enough to kill him."

"There it is," John thought. "He always mentions Billington." He put his hand up to his face, trying to keep the thought from showing.

The governor wasn't looking at his son. He shook his head. "'Tis in God's hands. Unless the man who shot Newcomen confesses for the sake of his own immortal soul, we may never find him out."

He pushed his still-full trencher away. "The reverend will lead prayers all day tomorrow asking God to lead the murderer forward, but I doubt that whoever it be is a God-fearing man, or he'd never have done this terrible thing." He got up from the bench and went into the other room.

"Perhaps thy father can find comfort in the Bible tonight if he does not go to Elder Brewster," John's stepmother said quietly. "Thou should go and read with him, John. He'll like that."

"It will do no good. He won't even notice I'm there," John said, but as soon as he'd finished clearing up, he picked up a book and went to sit on a stool by his father's chair.

His father had a library of many books. Only Elder Brewster had more. Like the governor, Elder Brewster was a scholar. He'd even written books and printed them when the Old Comers were in Holland. John knew that Elder Brewster was the man in the colony his father most respected. Both men could read in many languages: Dutch, German, Latin, Greek, and several others. John could speak Dutch, and Reverend Robinson had taught him Latin, but he was comfortable only in English.

Just as John had predicted, his father failed to pay him any mind. John glanced up at his father often as the evening passed. The governor was staring at the Bible he held in front of him, but his eyes were not moving down the page. He sighed deeply and often. After a while, without a word to anyone, the governor closed his book and went across the street to the Brewster house.

He went there often, or Elder Brewster would come

to their house. Elder Brewster sometimes joined the governor in conducting John's lessons. That always made John doubly nervous, although Elder Brewster was more patient than the governor.

Now John thought there must be something he could do—some little thing that would please the governor. He walked around the house, seeking something that would surprise his father and lift his mood. Coming back into the room where they'd been reading, John noticed the piles of books stacked up near his father's chair.

How could the governor find what he wanted in such disorder? Carefully, John sorted the books and placed them on the shelves, putting all the books in each language together. Languages he couldn't identify he placed on yet another shelf. There! It was a small thing, but it should please his father.

"John!"

His father's shout woke John the next morning. He stumbled down the loft ladder to see the governor, standing beside the bookshelves, hands on his hips, but there was no pleasure on his face.

"Did thou do this?" He waved his hand at the bookshelves.

"Aye." John was confused, struggling to come awake from his sound sleep.

"Why? Why would thou do such a thing?"

"To make . . . I wanted to . . ." John stammered, trying to find the words. "I thought they'd be easier for thee to find, Father," he finished lamely.

"Easier to find with the works by one author all mixed in with the works by another? With philosophy in the middle of the science books?"

"With each language separate, Father."

"Bah! Now I can find nothing."

"I shall put them back, Father."

"No! Leave it. Thou have done enough. I'll tend to it later when I've time." His father shook his head and left the house.

John turned to see his stepmother in the doorway, a sad smile on her face. Young William stood beside her, grinning at John's discomfort.

14

To Sea

"I'm to go where?"

John had been summoned to the meetinghouse to meet with his father and Elder Brewster. Knowing how angry his father had been about the books the day before, John had expected to be assigned some particularly unwelcome chore such as mucking out a beasthouse. He was sure his ears were deceiving him when he heard what the task was to be.

Elder Brewster repeated it. "Thou art to go to the trading post at Aptucxet, John."

"Me? Art thou sure?" John kept his eyes on Elder Brewster, after one nervous glance at his father's expressionless face.

Elder Brewster nodded. "Quite sure, John. Thanks to the Dutch, we have wampum and yard goods for trade. We need furs for the founders in England. The trip should be a good experience for thee."

"Alone?" John asked. It was a foolish question, and he regretted it as soon as he'd asked it. His father's glance showed his contempt for the idea. Of course they would not send him alone.

"Master Allerton will be in charge. Masters Alden and Howland are also going. And Hobbamuck. He wants to meet with Massasoit in a village near the trading post," Elder Brewster explained. "Ed Doty will help the crew when necessary," he added.

"Crew?" John asked. "We're going by boat?"

Another foolish question. His father grunted his disgust.

"Aye," Elder Brewster spoke. "'Tis faster, and we don't intend for it to take more than a few days."

It was hard for John to restrict himself to a nod when what he wanted to do was leap and shout. He'd be leaving the village for a while. Since the murder, the colonists had talked about little else. Not only that, the whole village now seemed closed up. Laughter and good times seemed to have been drained from it the night Newcomen's body was brought home. People looked at each other differently. They whispered behind their hands. Leaving Plymouth, the murder, and Rachel's illness behind even for a short while would be a great relief for John.

His father spoke for the first time. "Thou shall do what thou art told and only what thou art told, John. If thou go to the Wampanoag village with the others, be extra careful not to offend. We've worked hard to keep our peace with the Indians, and our trade is good for us and good for them. I'll not have anyone, least of all my son, do anything—anything, John—

to change that. Keep thy mouth closed. Do only what those who know what they are doing tell thee to do. Not one thing more, John. Watch. Listen. Learn."

John gulped and nodded. "I will, Father. I will."

Elder Brewster spoke. "Of course thou will, John. I have the utmost faith in thee." The fact that Elder Brewster had said that *he* had faith and not "*we* have faith" was not lost on John. Elder Brewster went on. "Pack warm clothes. 'Tis often cold on the boat, even this time of year, especially at night, and take food enough for four days, just in case there's a delay in getting back."

Governor Bradford had been watching his son carefully while these instructions were being given. His look was doubtful, and John was sure that sending him on this trip had not been his father's idea.

"When do I leave?" John asked.

"On tomorrow's tide," the governor answered.

"Thank thee," John said. He smiled broadly as he nodded to Elder Brewster. Then he looked solemnly at his father. "Thank thee, Father," he said and quickly left the room before his father could say more.

He stood for a moment outside the meetinghouse, unsure which thing to do first—rush to tell Sam? Run home to tell his stepmother?

The door behind him opened, and his father stepped out.

"John," he said, "perhaps I spoke harshly, but thou need to be aware of the importance of this errand."

"Art thou sure thou want me to go?" John asked. "Sam could . . ."

"'Twas my decision," his father said. He seemed about to say more but went back inside.

John sat on his rock by the sea a long time that evening before the sun went down as his initial joy changed to fear and doubt. His father did want him to go. That was comforting, but what if he managed to mess things up again?

Would he be meeting Massasoit? What would he say to the great leader? The wrong thing, no doubt. All the stories he had heard about Massasoit ran through his head. People said that Massasoit was quick to take offense. What if John did offend him somehow? Would he know that John was the governor's son? No doubt Hobbamuck would tell him. Would Massasoit expect John to be like his father? If things did go wrong, and it was John's fault, his father would never forgive him.

John could pretend he was sick. Indeed, his stomach was queasy enough to make that almost a fact. But sickness was weakness, and his father would see it that way. John remembered a time when the gov-

ernor was down with a cough so bad they feared for
his life, yet the governor had risen from his sickbed
when a group of Indians came to talk with him.

Thinking of sickness made John recall his seasickness on board the *Talbot* when he came to Plymouth.
It had laid him low for days. Almost all the passen-
gers had been sick on the voyage, so there was no disgrace in it, but what if he was overcome with the
seasickness this time? The crew would surely not fall
victim to it. Master Allerton had been back and forth
to England several times as well as up and down the
coast. He would not fall ill. John didn't know about
the seaworthiness of the others. What if they were all
good sailors, and he was not? Such thoughts were
leading him nowhere. He walked slowly home and
went to bed.

Sleep didn't come, and as the night wore on, John
invented and discarded one scheme after another as
reasons not to go on the journey. In the morning a
pale and heavy-lidded John stepped into the rowboat
to be taken to the ship. His spare clothes were
wrapped around the food his stepmother had pre-
pared for him, making a sort of sack.

He looked back to see Rachel standing on the
shore. Her hand was up near her shoulder almost as
if she were waving, John thought, but it might have

been just to steady Spy. Nevertheless he waved to her before turning to face the ship.

He'd seen the little ship before. It was not oceangoing, but the colonists used it for trade up and down the coast from all the way up in Maine to the Connecticut River. It had one deck, a square stern, and two masts.

"Welcome aboard, John," Master Allerton said as he stretched out his hand to help John out of the rowboat. John took his hand but staggered and nearly fell as he stepped over the rail. He came within an inch of dropping his clothing sack into the water. He righted himself quickly and hoped no one had noticed his awkwardness.

"Put yer gear down here," Ed Doty said, leading John down a ladder to the hold. "Though ye'll want to be on deck unless there's a storm."

A storm. John hadn't even thought of the possibility of a storm. He gulped as he climbed down into the hold. Even with the small amount of light that came through the open hatch, John could see that this hold was much cleaner than the *Talbot*'s was. Still, that hold had been clean enough at the beginning of the voyage. The filth and the stench had come gradually over the long days and nights at sea. He put his sack far to the side and then followed Ed back up on deck.

Apparently, John was the last to board; the crew

immediately got to work hoisting sails. Almost as soon as the sails were in place, the wind caught them, the anchor was hoisted, and the boat glided forward.

John leaned against the rail, watching the waves as the ship turned out to sea. There was a slight up-and-down motion as the waves hit the prow. John stayed apart from the others as he waited for the first signs of seasickness, vowing not to show it when it came.

He looked to his left to see Hobbamuck also leaning against the rail. He looked no happier than John.

Master Allerton walked toward John. "Ye'll be fine, John," he said. "'Tis a short trip, and we'll not be out of sight of land. We won't hit much stronger seas than this. Keep yer eye on the horizon till ye get the hang of it." John noticed that Master Allerton spoke loudly enough for Hobbamuck to overhear.

John nodded gratefully. "How long will it take?" he asked. He wasn't sure how long he'd be able to keep his stomach down. He hadn't eaten breakfast, and that may not have been a good thing.

Master Allerton handed John a hunk of cornbread. "Eat this slowly," he said. "'Twill help."

He stepped over to Hobbamuck and held out another piece of bread. "Want to try it?" he asked.

Hobbamuck nodded his thanks and took the bread. A few moments later Hobbamuck moved closer to John.

"Won't be a long trip, they say," Hobbamuck said. In spite of his queasiness, John grinned. Hobbamuck must be feeling a bit seasick himself.

"Shouldn't take us more than one day going, one day there, and one day coming back," Master Allerton said. "Keep yer eyes on the horizon," he added as he walked away.

Hobbamuck smiled and repeated the words. "Eyes on the horizon, John."

"Think it will help?" John asked.

Hobbamuck shrugged. "Who can tell?"

It wasn't long before the ship changed course and headed south. John felt his stomach lurch as the waves began to rock the boat from side to side. Hobbamuck walked to the starboard side and leaned over the rail there. John followed. It was easier to keep his eye on the horizon when it was land he stared at instead of the ever moving open sea.

That did seem to help and, gradually, John was able to relax a bit. Hobbamuck seemed to feel better, too. He left the rail but stood apart from Masters Allerton, Howland, and Alden, who were deep in conversation at the stern. Ed Doty had helped the crew with the sails and was now to John's left with his back up against the rail, gazing up at the sky.

He then motioned to John, and John walked toward him, trying to keep his gait in rhythm with the roll. He stumbled a bit, but Ed didn't seem to notice.

"Care for a game?" Ed asked. He made lines on the deck for Nine Men's Morris with a piece of chalk.

John quickly knelt beside the diagram. "I'll take white," he said, grateful for the diversion.

From a small bag Ed took the nine white stones and nine black ones and laid them out.

They were so absorbed in the game that it wasn't until they heard the crew's shouts and the flapping of the ropes that the boys looked up to see that the sky had darkened. The stones began to roll across the deck. The ship was now swaying from side to side as large waves hit the port side. The sails flapped noisily as the wind gusted, rattling the ropes against the deck and masts.

"Oh my," John said as Ed scooped up the stones and put them back in the bag.

"Doty here! Others get below!" shouted one of the crew, and John followed the others down the ladder. The hatch was slammed shut, and they were in almost complete darkness. John felt his way along the floor of the hold. He tried to sit with his back against the side, but the ship continued to roll from side to side. He scrambled to grab anything that would keep him in place.

A few minutes later the hatch opened, and a large

amount of water poured down upon them as a voice called, "All hands on deck!"

Water continued to splash over them as they climbed the ladder. The deck was awash with water, and they struggled to keep their footing on a deck that tilted dangerously from one direction to the next. John clung to the rail as the boat tilted so far that his feet dangled in the air behind him.

The crew were taking down sail as fast as they could, yelling orders over their shoulders as they worked. Master Allerton and the other men struggled to help. One sailor yelled at Ed Doty to grab hold of a sail. He did so just as the ship heeled sharply. A large wave surged over the boat, and John saw a helpless Doty washed up over the rail and into the sea. It happened so quickly that Ed had no time to yell.

John hollered, "Man overboard! Help him! Help him!" No one seemed to hear or to be aware of what had happened. John looked around for something—anything—big enough to grab hold of that would float.

A broken piece of timber was sliding about with each roll of the boat. John grabbed the end of a rope and wrapped it around the timber, securing it with a knot that he hoped would hold.

He looked over the rail for any sign of Ed. At first

there was nothing, and then Ed's head appeared not far off the side where John stood. Holding to the rail with one arm, John pitched the wood as far as he could in that direction. The wind was against him, and the board plopped down uselessly, close to the boat. Desperately John hauled the timber back as he watched Ed's head disappear beneath the waves.

Just as John pulled back his arm to throw again, Hobbamuck grabbed one end of the board, allowing John to grasp the other. Together they heaved the board farther out. They kept hold of the end of the rope with their other hands, grasping the rail as they searched the waves for a sign of Ed. As Doty's head appeared, John shouted, "Grab hold! Grab hold!" His shout was lost in the wind. Hobbamuck shouted, "Over there! Grab the wood!" The Indian's deeper voice seemed to carry. As the next wave took him in the right direction, Ed saw the timber and took hold of it. By this time, Masters Howland and Allerton had each taken hold of the rope, and they dragged Ed up and over the rail. There he dangled, head down.

"Well done," Master Allerton said, clapping John and Hobbamuck on the back as the others tended to the exhausted servant, who now lay gasping against the rail, his eyes toward John.

John nodded, holding tight to the rail, too exhausted and relieved to speak.

"A close one," Hobbamuck said.

A few minutes later, the squall ceased as suddenly as it began, the sky cleared, and the wind settled down to merely brisk.

Soon the ship changed course again, and they neared land at the mouth of the Scusset River. A few minutes of fairly rough water got them past the mouth and on to the smooth passage of the river.

Ed Doty seemed to recover from his dousing with no ill effects. He thanked everybody for his rescue, saving his loudest thanks for John and Hobbamuck.

"Until I saw that board there," he said, "I thought sure I was a goner."

All but Hobbamuck joined in prayers of thanks. John thought his own prayer was probably as heart-felt as Ed's. At least this was one time he had not messed things up.

All too soon that part of the trip was over. The crew lowered a rowboat, and after the yard goods and wampum were loaded into it, John joined the others in the brief trip to shore. John fingered the wampum. It looked nothing like English or Dutch money. He wondered how the strings of polished shells came to be used as currency.

Master Allerton grinned when he saw what John was doing. "Be grateful for those shells, John," he said. "They changed everything."

"Really? How?" John asked.

"We got them from the Dutch. They got them from the Indians. The Indians here will pay furs for wampum. With that wampum, we can get furs to send back to England."

All took their share of the load for the two-mile portage to the Manomet River, where another row-boat was waiting. Then Master Alden took the oars for the brief row up that river to the trading post called Aptucxet.

Aptucxet was a surprise. John had expected it to look like the shops in Holland, but it was a small one-room building on the south side of the river. He thought they'd be dealing with Indians, but the man who greeted them was no Indian.

He was the biggest man John had ever seen—at least six feet tall, John thought, and fat. The man's potbelly made gaps between the buttons of his shirt. His long, gray hair looked as though it had never felt a comb. He brushed it back out of his eyes as he welcomed them.

"Tom Clarke at yer service," he said, stretching out his hand to John Alden as he stepped to shore. He greeted each of the others in turn and then led all except Hobbamuck into the post, where he introduced the other post men. Hobbamuck sat on the riverbank.

"Got a fine lot for ye this time," Tom Clarke said, waving his hand toward a pile of furs that lay on the counter. Everything he said seemed to hold as much laughter as talk.

Isaac Allerton went over to examine the furs as John Howland approached one of the other men.

Tom Clarke walked over to Ed Doty. "Bondservant?" he asked as Ed finished unloading the boat.

"Aye," Ed answered.

"Who's this?"

Ed smiled. "This is John Bradford. He and Hobbamuck saved my life."

Tom Clarke looked John up and down. "Did he now?" He cocked his head. "Bradford, ye said. The governor's son?"

John nodded.

"That can't be easy," Tom Clarke said. After a long look at John, Tom turned his attention back to Ed Doty.

"How many years yet?" he asked.

"Two."

"Staying when it's over?"

"Aye."

"Good. 'Tis the only way our like can gain a footing." Tom Clarke clapped his hand on Ed's shoulder. "I did the same."

"Ye were bonded?" John Bradford asked.

"Aye," he said. "I'd no land, no money for passage."

"Wouldn't ye rather be in Plymouth?" Ed Doty asked. "It must be lonely here."

"Thought I'd die when I first saw this place," Tom Clarke said. "I was a city boy. Raised in York. I'd thought I would be in Plymouth, and that was bad enough, but here there was nothing but trees and savages and a couple of other bondservants like me. Cried like a baby, I did. Now I wouldn't go to Plymouth if ye paid me. All those people!" He shivered. "Even here they're getting closer all the times. Folks all up and down the coast now."

"But what is there to do here?" John asked.

"Very little, my boy, very little, and that's the beauty of it." Tom Clarke motioned toward the woods. "People come, but they also go. There's no one to tell us what to do. We must grow corn and raise pigs. Other than that, as long as we're here when the boats arrive, or the Indians come, no one cares what we do." He grinned and scratched his chest. "We hunt a little, fish a little, dream a lot, and drink a lot. The Indians are good company, once they learn to trust ye. 'Tis a fine life." He turned to speak to Ed. "Ye might think on it yerself when yer years are done up there in the big city."

Several Indians came to the trading post. They all

stopped to talk with Hobbamuck in a language John could make neither head nor tail of. As always, John was shocked at how little the Indian men wore in the summer—mainly loincloths. They paid little attention to the settlers.

As John and the others loaded up the boat, he looked back at Tom Clarke, as he and the other post men talked with the Indians. Although Tom had suggested Ed for the job, John thought he might be better off here himself. Certainly he'd be far enough away from his father to escape the daily disapproval.

When the boat was loaded and secured, they made their beds on the floor of the trading post. The next morning Hobbamuck led them to a path through the forest at the edge of the river. The path was well used and quite wide, unlike the paths in the woods near Plymouth. After about a half mile, John could smell food cooking and hear voices. Coming around the bend, he saw the first of many circular wetus like the one Hobbamuck lived in. Some were larger than others and covered with bark. Smaller ones had cattail coverings. Indian women were cooking over a fire in the middle of the village. There was a group of men sitting at the far edge.

The adult Indians ignored the visitors after a quick glance in their direction, but the children stopped their play and stared openly.

Then a man stepped out of a wetu. There was little to distinguish him from any other of the men in the village except for a chain of white beads.

John was not surprised to hear Ed Doty whisper, "'Tis Massasoit."

"Stay here," Master Allerton said to John and Ed, as he and the other men went to where Massasoit stood waiting. John smiled his relief. He'd be glad to keep his distance. There'd be no chance of his offending Massasoit this way. The men spoke briefly with Massasoit before most of them returned to John and Ed. Hobbamuck stayed to talk with Massasoit while the others walked slowly back to the boat.

On the trip home John wondered what his father would say when he heard about the storm and Ed's rescue. John vowed not to tell his father himself lest his father accuse him again of being prideful. Let the news get to his father the way everything else did.

If John had expected words of great praise from his father, however, he was to be disappointed. The day after their return, as the governor sat down to breakfast, he asked of no one in particular, "Is Doty any the worse for wear?"

So he had heard about the incident. John's head popped up.

One of the other men at the table answered, "Seemed right as rain last evening."

A nod from the governor ended the discussion.

Later that night, when John was in the loft, he heard Master Kempton say, "Seems John did himself well on the trip to Aptucxet."

John scrambled over to the edge of the loft to hear what his father said.

"Aye," said the governor. "So did Hobbamuck."

"Ed Doty sings his praises."

"He's a good lad," John's stepmother said.

"Agree, Father," John said to himself. "Agree. 'Yes, he is a good lad.' Say it, Father." But that was the end of the conversation.

15

Lost

John was surprised a week later when, at mid-morning, Rachel came to the far field and sat near him, watching as he hoed the corn. Sam was at work in the Eaton field, just a short distance away. He looked up and waved.

Spy hopped down from Rachel's shoulder and searched the overturned earth, being careful to stay out of John's way.

"I've got to admit thou has trained Spy well, Rachel," John said. "That's a well-mannered crow."

He thought there might have been the slightest trace of a smile on the child's face, but it disappeared in an instant, and her usual sad look was back.

"Rachel," he said, encouraged by that momentary change of expression. "I thought thou were teaching Spy to talk. She'll never learn unless thou speak to her."

He waited, but Rachel gave no sign that she had heard. John went back to work. When he looked up again, she was gone.

In late afternoon, he stopped for a minute at the Howland house to watch Master Howland tearing off the burned clapboards. More were damaged than John had realized. No doubt the community would get together soon to help him repair it.

Rachel came up behind him as John slowed his walk.

"Rachel," he said, turning to face her. "Talk to me."

Tears ran down her face as she slowly shook her head.

Rachel went into her house as Sam came up the street. "Thank thee for trying, John," he said.

John nodded. He stopped at the Fuller house and picked up the leftover clapboards and continued toward his own house. He placed the clapboards carefully on the lean-to pile at the rear.

John was exhausted from field work, and his thoughts were about Rachel that evening. He hadn't been listening to the conversation between his father and the others until he heard his stepmother ask if there was any progress in the investigation.

His father said there was none, that those who had gone to Massachusetts Bay Colony had come back with no new information or suspicions. Governor Winthrop had promised to conduct his own investigation.

Allerton and the other men had talked with Massasoit, his father said. They knew that if an Indian had been involved, Massasoit would know. He had heard about the murder, but none of his people had seen anything.

"Massasoit asked if the drunken one did it," his father said. "He means Billington, of course. Even the Indians know him for the drunken fool he is."

John stiffened but held his tongue.

"Hobbamuck tells them, I suppose," his stepmother observed.

"There's not much that goes on here that Massasoit doesn't know," the governor answered.

"But thou don't think it was Billington, surely."

"It could have been," his father said. "The man is capable of almost anything when he's drunk."

John could stand it no longer. He jumped up. "He didn't do it! He told thee he didn't do it! Thou blame him for everything!"

John knew he was shouting, but he couldn't stop. His father had leaped to his feet, his face red and his eyes wide. He placed both fists on the table and leaned toward John, ready to speak.

"John," his stepmother said. "John, don't—"

But John couldn't stop. "He's just like me! He tries to please thee, but he can do nothing right! Thou left me behind in Holland for years. Thou never wanted me here. Not me and not John Billington. We're both outcasts. Just put us both on a boat and cast us out like Morton. The colony would be better off without either of us. That way thou can pretend we were never born. Not Billington and not me!"

His father was still struggling to speak as John ran from the house. His feet seemed hardly to touch the ground as he flew down The Highway and into the woods. He was crying hard, bumping into trees, bouncing back, and running on.

When he did stop, too tired to do anything but sink to the ground, he could feel blood dripping down his face. He must have hurt himself somehow. Maybe he was badly hurt. He could bleed to death out here and no one would care. Breathing hard from his run, John put his hand to his forehead and gently touched the wound. He was almost disappointed to find it was just a small cut. He leaned back against the trunk of a tree and considered what had happened.

He'd done it now. His father would never forgive him. God wouldn't forgive him either. "Honor thy father and mother," the Bible said. John would never find grace in the eyes of God now. He couldn't be one of God's Chosen Ones. He'd shouted at his father.

John could scarcely remember the words he'd used. He'd cast his lot with Billington; he knew that. Why? What did it matter? Except for that one time in the forest when Master Billington had fixed Spy's wing and the time when he'd been so drunk, John had had nothing to do with the man. Why did he care so much what his father thought of John Billington?

His father had said nothing about John's trip to Aptucxet. That was a time his father should have been proud of him and said so, but he had not. It was one more way that his father had shown that he cared nothing for his son. Other fathers would be bragging about their son's bravery and resourcefulness in a time of such danger, but not Governor Bradford. John might as well be a Billington for all the respect he got.

John slapped at a mosquito he felt on his forehead and winced. The cut on his head began to bleed again.

Night air was dangerous. He could fall ill. Soon the pale sliver of a moon would give the only light. He was hungry and wished he'd eaten more before his outburst. How long did it take a person to starve to death? Sam could bring him food, but Sam would never find him. No one else would, either.

John looked around. Nothing seemed familiar. How far had he run? It seemed like miles. Which way had he run? South, wasn't it? The ocean should be over there somewhere. He could walk east to the ocean and find his way to Plymouth by walking north along the shore. But he couldn't go home.

Maybe he could sneak back into the village, find Sam, get some food, and then go on to the north—

to Massachusetts Bay. Surely they'd take him in. They took in Morton, didn't they?

John stood and headed in the direction he hoped was east. When he could no longer put one foot in front of the other, he sat down in a clearing, put his back up against a small tree, and listened. He should be able to hear the ocean by now, but he did not. Maybe he was miles from the ocean. Maybe he'd been heading the wrong way.

His stepmother must be worried. She would care what happened to him, even if his father did not. John was sorry to worry her. Perhaps she'd convince his father to send out searchers. That was a comforting thought. It would be shameful to be brought back by searchers, but better than starving to death in the woods.

He must have slept a bit. When he opened his eyes, a few birds were chirping. It must be almost dawn. In daylight he'd be able to find his own way home. If he came across searchers, he'd hide.

He looked back in the direction he'd come. It looked lighter where he could see a bit of sky. Was that east? Had he been traveling west all this time? To the west of Plymouth was the wild land. If he'd been heading west, he was miles away from home now and hopelessly lost.

Wait! Maybe he hadn't come from that direction.

He might have come into the clearing from over by that rock.

He listened again. He heard no sound of the surf, but he did hear footsteps—slow, careful footsteps. Searchers! They were looking for him.

He jumped up and hollered, "Over here! I'm over here. 'Tis me! John Billington!" He gasped. Had he really said that? He shouted again. "I mean John Bradford. I'm John Bradford!" There was a crashing noise in the brush and then silence—not searchers then but some wild beast he'd frightened off.

He sat down again. Even if they did send out searchers, would anyone be able to find him? They'd found Newcomen, but not until he was dead. What if the night air had sickened him? John could be dead by the time they found him. What if the killer was out here now, looking for John this time?

He sank back against the tree. He was too tired even to be scared. He should get up and find his way, but he was so tired—so very tired. He prayed briefly, closed his eyes, and slept.

He awakened to the squawk of a crow and a push on his shoulder.

John opened his eyes to see Rachel standing beside him, Spy at her feet.

"Rachel," he said. "How did thou . . . What art thou doing way out here?" Birds were flying about in the tops of the trees. A woodpecker hammered on the trunk of an oak.

"Is Plymouth very far away?" he asked. "Did thou run away too, Rachel?"

She pulled at John's arms until he got up. Spy squawked and began walking toward some blueberry bushes. John followed Rachel around the bushes. He was surprised to be at the edge of the far fields.

"Oh," he said, feeling very foolish.

Sam looked up, waved, and went back to work. Two men were working at another field, and he could see some others heading to the brook with fishing poles. There must have been no alarm about his running away. No search was organized. No one seemed surprised to see John. He turned to thank Rachel, but she was gone. John headed home.

"Were thou truly in the woods all night?" Sam asked. "No alarm was put out."

"Nay," John said. "They didn't tell anyone I was gone, I think. Too ashamed, I guess."

This walk down to the brook to fish was the first chance the boys had had to be together for several days.

"Weren't thou afraid of wild beasts?"

John shook his head. "I was too angry and then too tired to be scared."

"What did thy father say?"

"Nothing then and nothing since."

"He's not angry with thee for running away? For daring to yell at him?"

John shrugged. "I don't think he cares enough to be angry. He ignores me. I could be a hook on the wall for all the attention he pays me. He didn't even say anything about Ed Doty and the trip."

Sam said, "Well, he ought to be proud of what thou did there, John. Ed talks about it all the time."

They reached the brook and walked to where the calmer water formed pools among the rocks.

"Maybe 'tis just as well that thy father doesn't speak to thee right now," Sam said. He stopped where large willow bushes spread down almost to the water. Pushing through the branches, he reached into his pocket for an earthworm, baited the hook, and lowered the line. There was a soft plunk as the hook hit the water's surface.

"Thou might not like to hear what he would say after such an outburst." Sam picked out a spot beneath the tree and sat down.

John nodded slightly in agreement as he stooped to look for a bug to bait his own hook.

"Thy stepmother," Sam said. He pulled his line up a bit and then lowered it, letting the hook drag along the bottom. "Does she speak?"

"Aye."

"What does she say?" Sam asked.

John shrugged. "She said I had saddened her by speaking to my father that way." He turned over a rock with his foot, startling a beetle. He made a grab for it, but it scurried away. Two other beetles, too small for bait, weren't as quick as the first. John watched as they hid under a leaf.

"She said I'd best work it out with God. She said she'd talk to me about it after I'd prayed. It will come right with her, I know. 'Tis my father. He's the hard one."

"Perhaps there's something thou could do to please him."

"I tried, Sam, but it always goes wrong. If I pour him beer, I spill it. I say something that I know he'll agree with, and it comes out wrong. And he spends hours telling me how wrong it was. I went on the search, and embarrassed both of us by getting hurt. I rearranged his books, and he hated it. I helped to save Ed Doty's life, and I might as well have tried to drown him for all my father cares. I have been trying to please him since the day I arrived here. For two long years, Sam!" John put down his pole and sat down on the rock, his head between his hands. "Everything comes out wrong."

He picked a broad leaf, held it edgewise between

his thumbs, and blew on it, making it whistle.

"If only he'd talk to me," he went on, throwing down the leaf. "I'd rather be scolded. Whipped, even. Anything's better than this awful silence."

"He's a good man," Sam said.

"I know he's a good man. Everyone knows he's a good man. That's half the problem. The other half is me."

"It will work out, John," Sam said.

16

Explanation

"Go to him," John's stepmother said that evening when the dishes were done up and the younger children were in bed.

John looked up from the book he had just opened. Supper had been a solemn affair, as were most of the meals lately; only the women's soft murmurs or the chatter of the children broke the silence.

John had given up speaking any more than absolutely necessary when his father was present, reluctant to draw even a glance from the man from whom anger seemed ready to erupt at any moment.

This evening the governor had left the table as soon as he'd eaten. He was sitting on the bench just outside the open door.

"Go to him?" John asked incredulously. He spoke softly to keep his father from hearing. "Go to him?" He repeated the question as he motioned toward the doorway and lowered his voice still more. "Out there?"

His stepmother nodded.

"Surely not." John backed away, shaking his head. He moved to the other side of the room, as far as possible from the doorway. Still he whispered. "Father doesn't want to see me even when things are good.

Soon he'll go over to Elder Brewster's. Until then, I'm sure he'd rather be alone. Or with thee," John said, suddenly inspired. Taking his stepmother's arm, he pulled on it gently, urging her toward the door. "Thou should go to him. Thou can always make things better with him."

"Not this time," she said, removing John's hand from her arm. "Only thou can mend it this time, John. Go to him."

"But he'll be furious," John said. "He hates me."

She shook her head. "He loves thee, John. Speak to him."

"What shall I say?"

"Tell him how thou feeleth."

"About what?"

"About everything. About being here in Plymouth. About being his son."

John's eyes were wide at the thought. "Tell my father that he shouldn't have left me behind in Holland? Tell him that I'm trying to please him?" He gasped. "I cannot. I cannot." John shivered at the thought of saying such things to his father. He could just imagine his father's wrath. "No," he repeated. "I cannot."

He went into the other room and picked up a book. When he climbed the ladder to the loft later, there was no sign of his father or stepmother.

The next morning when John climbed down from the loft, his father sat alone at the table.

"Good morrow, Father," John said. He looked quickly around for the others, but there was no sign of them.

"Sit, John." His father pointed to a stool.

John sat, squeezing his hands between his knees to keep them from shaking.

"Father," he said. He kept his head down. He couldn't bear to look at his father's face. "I'm sorry." He started to get up and then thought the better of it. "I'm sorry I yelled. I'm sorry I ran off. I'm sorry . . ." He struggled through the long list in his head of all the things he was sorry for. There were too many. "I'm sorry," he repeated. He stared at the floor, waiting for his father to speak. When he did not, John looked up.

His father nodded. There was a moment where the two held each other's glance. Then his father spoke.

"Sorry indeed," he said. "Your mother hardly slept that night for the worry of thee. 'Twas needless and thoughtless to worry her so."

His father turned his gaze from John's face and spoke looking down at the table. "I thought thee understood how it was that thou were left behind in Holland, John. Thy birth was a hard one, leaving both thee and thy mother weak. Thou were too sickly to make the journey first back to England and then here. I should have insisted that she stay back as well as thee."

"My own mother, thou mean," John said.

"Aye," said his father. He cleared his throat. "We decided to leave thee with the Robinsons until things were settled here. We knew thou would have a home. Reverend Robinson was a good and learned man, and thy home would be right in the church. We put thee in his care, and we came to America. Then thy mother died." There was a long pause during which both John and his father sat with their heads down. His father looked up and continued. "It wasn't long after her death that the sickness came, and others began to die. So many, John, so many died that winter." For a moment he seemed overcome with the sadness of the memory. "I was glad then that thou were spared—that thou couldn't be touched with it."

"And when the sickness was over . . ." John said.

His father took up the sentence without hesitation. "When the sickness was over, there was no one who could care for a sickly two-year-old motherless child. Most of the women were gone, and those few who were left had all the other children to care for. In Holland thou had a home, a good family to care for thee. Here there was need and work—so much work that needed to be done, and so few of us to do it."

John nodded. He was going to say nothing, but then he had to speak. "That was the first year, Father. I grew strong in Holland. I know I was strong enough to come many years ago."

"Strong enough to come perhaps, but not strong enough to work. I could not call for thee, John." His father shook his head. "We used what little money we had to bring able souls here to work for the good of the community. What work could a two-year-old do? The sponsors in England demanded their share."

"Thou sent for my stepmother."

"I did," his father nodded. "She was strong, able to contribute to the colony, able to bear children. We'd lost so many. We had to increase our numbers." He stood and walked toward the door, then turned and faced his son. "I had to act for the good of the colony. We all did. There were many who sacrificed, John. Ours was nothing in comparison."

John nodded. "I know there was great sacrifice, but I . . ."

"But nothing," said his father, cutting John off. If there had been a trace of softness in the governor's face and voice, it was gone now. He took two steps toward John. "I've explained how it was and the reasons for my decision. Thou art nearly twelve years of age. The Bible says, 'When I was a child, I spake as a child, I understood as a child, I thought as a child: but when I became a man, I put away childish things.'"

"But I have put them away," John protested. "I have behaved like a man. On the trip to Aptucxet I saved Doty's life, and thou didn't even . . ."

"Even what, John? Praise thee for it?"

"Aye." John stood and almost shouted the word. Then more softly: "Or at least say that it was a good thing."

His father's expression was one of disappointment. "Thou knew it was a good thing. My saying so was unnecessary. I praised God, John. I praised Him for using thee and Hobbamuck as instruments of His will. If thou helped to save Doty's life in order to be praised, 'twas a sinful act of vanity—and a childish aim."

"But nothing I do is good enough," John protested. "I just want—"

His father interrupted. "It is not my task to give thee what thou want. It is my task to help thee to be right with God, to educate thee, to see that thou have food and shelter when there is food and shelter to be had. Other than that, my eyes are on the heavens and then on the community. Make of that what thou will."

He drew a deep breath and walked to the door

before turning to face his son. "'Tis time to put the acts of a child away, John. Time to stop running away. Time to turn from a need for praise. What was —was. Only the man thou will become is in thy power. Put thy thoughts and thy actions toward that time. Get ready, John. 'Tis time to get on with it." The governor turned and left the house, shutting the door firmly behind him.

17

A Whisper

Sam and John were gathering brush for kindling the next morning.

"And then what happened?" Sam asked, placing one foot at the base of a fallen branch as he whacked off the smaller branches with his hatchet.

"Nothing," John said. "Nothing happened. He left, and I didn't see him again until evening prayers."

"What did he say then?"

"'Let us pray,'" John said. He picked up another stick, broke it in two, and added it to his pile.

Sam chuckled. "Very funny. But nothing changed? He didn't treat thee differently?"

John shook his head. He spoke over his shoulder as he headed for another fallen branch. "He scolded me for fidgeting during prayers." John turned back toward his friend. "He's not going to change. If there are any changes, they won't come from my father."

Sam nodded. He tied up his bundle of branches and pulled it up onto his back.

"I saw Master Billington coming back to the village last night," Sam said, changing the subject. "He was very drunk. Folks would respect him more if he drank less."

John shook his head. "Folks won't respect John

Billington no matter what he does. Once they get set on someone, there it stays. Believe me. I know."

He sat down on a large rock. There was a rustling noise behind him, and Spy hopped up beside him.

Sam turned and smiled, knowing Rachel couldn't be far away. When she appeared beside her pet, Sam asked, "Come to help us gather wood, Rachel?"

Rachel ignored her brother and went over to John. She put her hand on his shoulder. John looked from her hand to Sam and back again. Sam's eyes were on his sister's face. John smiled. It was wonderful to see Rachel getting back to her old self. She wasn't speaking yet, but she was moving around and getting close to people again.

Rachel remained by John's side. She took her hand from his shoulder and then put it back again. With John perched on the rock, she was eye to eye with him. She opened her lips as if to speak and then closed them again.

"What is it, Rachel?" he asked softly. "What is it thou want to say?"

For a very long minute she continued to stare at John. And then she spoke.

"He did it," Rachel whispered, looking from Sam to John.

"Rachel!" both boys spoke at once, and she jumped back, startled.

Sam put down his bundle and knelt beside his sister. He brushed one strand of hair off her face. He smiled. "Oh, Rachel," he said. "I didn't mean to scare thee, but 'tis so good to hear thy voice."

Rachel seemed unaware of his touch. She stood with her hands clasped in front, her eyes wide and full of tears. Her feet moved from side to side as if uncertain whether to go or stay. She opened her mouth as if to speak again, but threw herself into Sam's arms and sobbed, her head thrust into his shoulder.

Sam patted his sister gently on the back as she cried. Spy fluttered up to Sam's shoulder and waited, her head cocked. When at last Rachel pulled back, wiping her eyes on her shirt, Spy hopped over to her shoulder.

After his initial outburst, John had stood there silently watching Rachel. Now he spoke. "Who did, Rachel? Who did what?"

Again it was a whisper. "Master Billington."

"Master Billington?" Sam asked. "What did he do?"

The tears began to flow again. "Shot the man."

"Oh, Rachel," Sam said. He reached out for her, but she stepped back.

"Master Billington shot the man." Her voice was still soft but it was no longer a whisper.

"Rachel." Sam also spoke softly, wary of frightening his sister. "Some people say it was Master Billington, but 'tis just talk. Thou mustn't be upset. John and I know he didn't do it," Sam said.

Rachel shook her head rapidly, tears continuing to stream down her face. Then, with a loud gasp, she turned and ran. Spy fell from his perch on her shoulder and ran after her.

For a few minutes the boys said nothing, staring after Rachel.

When Sam spoke, his tone was one of relief. "My mother and father are going to be so glad that she's speaking again," Sam said. He grinned, his brow unwrinkled as it hadn't been since Rachel had begun her silence. He picked up his bundle and slung it over his back as they started home.

"She truly thinks Master Billington is the killer," John said. He was less cheered than Sam.

"She's confused. She hardly knows what she's saying," Sam said. "I'm just so glad to hear her speak; I don't care what she says."

"If she thinks Master Billington did it, no wonder she's been so upset," John said.

Sam nodded. "She's heard people talking, probably my father and thine. Thou know how many will blame Billingtons for anything. People talk. They don't notice that she's there, especially since she hasn't been speaking. They wouldn't care even if they did notice her. They say things."

"To be in such a state for so long. Poor thing." John shook his head.

"She's so flighty. It doesn't take much to get her upset," Sam said. He turned to John and grinned. "At least the silence is over. Let's hope 'tis the beginning of a whole stream of chatter. Praise be to God." He turned to go into his house. "Could it have been the ash twig, John?"

John shifted around a bit. Talk of the charm made him uneasy. "I don't know," he said. "I doubt it."

"I checked for it the next day and 'twas gone," Sam said. "Well, no matter. She's speaking at least."

"Aye," John agreed. "But what a thing to say."

18

Confession

When John stepped out of the house the next morning, he was surprised to see Sam there, holding Rachel by the hand. It was obvious by her wet face and swollen, red eyes that Rachel had been crying hard. Spy rubbed her beak against Rachel's face.

"We're going to find Master Billington," Sam said. "Come with us."

"Master Billington? Why?"

"Because Rachel still believes he killed John Newcomen."

Rachel's tears began again. "He did it," she said and began to sob.

Her brother continued, "We need to have Master Billington tell her that he did not. Then maybe she can stop crying."

"Rachel," John said. "'Tis just gossip thou heard. Master Billington told my father he didn't do it. No one lies to my father."

Rachel's face was devoid of expression, but the tears ran down. She shook her head.

"Come on then," John said. "If thou needs to hear it from the man himself, so be it." To Sam he said, "I just hope he's not drunk again."

They found Master Billington sitting down by the shore not far from where they had found him before.

"Is he drunk?" Sam whispered as they approached.

"Can't tell yet," John whispered back.

Without looking at the children, Billington spoke. "Storm's coming," he said. To their relief, his speech was not slurred.

John looked out to the horizon, where low clouds were forming. "Aye," he said. "It does look stormy."

"Master Billington," Sam said, clearing his throat. "We need ye to speak to Rachel."

A look of surprise came over Billington's face as he turned to look at Rachel, who had stopped a few feet back. She was looking down at her feet. Spy cocked her head and looked from the boys to the man.

Master Billington asked, "What would ye have me say?"

Sam said, "Well, Master Billington, ye see, Rachel has heard people talking, and she believes them when they say that ye . . . Well, that ye . . ."

Rachel looked straight at Master Billington and spoke over her brother's stammering. "Thou killed him," she said.

"Killed him?" Master Billington said. "They say I killed John Newcomen, and this little one thinks so too? What care I? Think what ye like, lass. Take yer fool crow and go gossip with the rest."

"We need ye to tell her it isn't true," John Bradford said.

Before Billington could speak, Rachel said again, "Thou killed him." She looked straight at John Billington, who shook his head.

"Nay, lass," he said. "I did not."

Rachel caught her breath and whispered, "I saw thee."

"Thou didn't see him, Rachel," Sam protested, but Master Billington's expression changed. He got up and went over to Rachel.

"Ye did not see it," Billington said, but he sounded unsure.

She was trying hard not to cry now. "I was up in a tree with Spy. I wanted her to fly. Thou came and I wanted Spy to fly down to thee for a surprise. Then the man came. He called thee a thief. He hit thee, and thou fell down." She stopped to wipe away tears. "And thou got up and shot him." She broke down completely then and sobbed, leaning against her brother's side.

Neither boy spoke as they looked from Rachel to Master Billington.

"Ye saw me." Master Billington put his hand on Rachel's shoulder and turned her toward him. "Me. Ye saw me shoot John Newcomen."

Rachel was crying too hard to do anything but nod.

"I was drunk."

"Ye–ye–yes," Rachel cried.

Master Billington seemed then to be speaking to the ground. "I was so drunk." He scuffed his foot in the dirt. "I remember seeing him in the woods. I remember the fight." He looked at the boys. "The next thing I remember was waking up in my own bed. I thought I'd dreamed it. Oh Lord! I thought I'd dreamed it."

The four stood there, the silence broken only by Rachel's sobs. Then Master Billington drew a deep breath and nodded. "Come with me," he said.

Sam and John shook their heads. "Nay," they said, speaking at once and drawing back.

"Come," Master Billington repeated. "We'll speak to the governor."

Without another word the children followed as John Billington led the way up The Street. The only sound apart from their footsteps was that of Rachel's sobs as she stumbled along, her face pressed against her brother's side.

Governor Bradford and Elder Brewster were seated on the bench outside the Bradford house. John's step-mother was on the ground beside them, mending a skirt. They all looked up as the solemn group approached.

"What is it?" the governor asked, standing up. "What's happened?"

Elder Brewster stood beside him. "Is someone hurt?" he asked as John's stepmother scrambled to her feet.

John Billington raised his face and looked directly at the governor. "I did it," he said. "I shot John Newcomen."

19

Resolution

Still sobbing loudly, Rachel was the first one to speak after Billington's confession. Her eyes were on him as she said, "Thou shalt not kill."

There was a rueful smile on Billington's face as he nodded. "Aye, lass," he said. "And had it not been for the drink, I'd never have done it."

He knelt in front of Rachel and wiped her tears with his handkerchief. "I never meant to do such a terrible thing."

It was as if there was no one else there as Billington spoke directly to Rachel.

"'Twas a foolish argument that went on and on," Master Billington continued. "No matter where we were or who was there, we argued every time we met. With all this land around us, we fought about a piece no bigger than a beasthouse." He shook his head. "We'd both had too much of the drink in us that day in the woods when we came upon each other and then . . . and then . . ."

He stood up and faced Governor Bradford and Elder Brewster. "I told myself I hadn't done it, that it was only the dreams of the drink that made me think I had."

"What made ye change yer mind?" Elder Brewster asked.

Billington pointed toward Rachel. "The child. She saw it. God help her," he said. "She saw me sin against man and God. I did it."

Governor Bradford reached out to grasp Billington's shoulder. "I'm sorry, Billington," he said. His voice was soft. He turned to Sam. "Take thy sister home. She needs a mother's care now."

"I'll go with thee," his wife said.

Sam nodded and took his sister's hand. John's stepmother put her arm around Rachel's shoulder, and they walked slowly away.

"What happens now?" John Billington asked. "Where do I go? What do I do?"

"Make peace with God," Elder Brewster said. "Take care of yer immortal soul."

"At home?" Billington asked. "Do I go to my house?"

"Aye," Governor Bradford said. "For now. Go home. Explain it, if ye can, to yer wife and son."

"Aren't ye afraid I'll run away?" Billington asked.

Governor Bradford shook his head. "If 'twas running ye had in mind, ye'd have run long ago."

"Aye," John Billington said. "There's no place to run from this."

John Bradford stood with his father and Elder Brewster as they watched Billington turn and leave. When John looked at his father's face, he saw it was wet with tears.

20
Aftermath

At noonday a few days later, John sat on his rock, looking out to sea, grateful once more for this place of peace. So much had happened so quickly, he needed time alone to think it out.

The whole community was shaken by John Billington's confession. Work, ordinarily done as a group effort, such as the repair of the Howland house, had been ignored. People talked in hushed tones as if another death had occurred. Opinions differed as to what should be done now.

No wonder poor Rachel had been wandering about in such a state. John prayed that Rachel could get past it somehow. He wished he knew a way to help her.

He also felt sorry for Master Billington, and he felt guilty about those thoughts. The man was a murderer. Murder was evil, but John didn't think Master Billington was an evil man.

And what was to become of Master Billington now? The governor had insisted on a trial, although others saw no point in it. Billington had confessed; what good was a trial? But Governor Bradford insisted, and Elder Brewster had agreed, that they must have a trial. This was a lawful community; they would go by the laws of England. A man accused of a crime would be tried by a jury of his peers.

This morning the jury was sitting at the meeting-house to hear whatever evidence there was. Rachel would probably have to testify. John hoped they'd allow Sam or her parents to be with her.

Too restless to sit still, John began to walk along the shore. He scuffed his feet along, scaring some hermit crabs that scuttled away. It was high tide and a large outcropping of rock came down almost to the water. He had to step carefully to keep from getting wet.

"Here's John."

John looked up to see Rachel and Sam sitting on a log on the other side of the outcrop. It was Sam who had spoken.

"What? Why? The trial . . ." John was too confused to finish the thought. He walked toward them up the beach.

Rachel got up quickly. She smiled slightly as she went by him down to the water with Spy.

"Good morrow, Rachel," he said. He turned to Sam. "The trial?"

"'Tis over," Sam said.

"Did Rachel . . . ?"

"No. Thy father fixed it so that she wouldn't have to testify."

"Is she all right?"

"No, not all right, but getting better. Each day she seems more and more like herself. She disappears with Spy for a while each evening, and when she comes back, she seems a little better each time. I think she comes down here."

John nodded. "There is peace here." He wished he had known that she was down here in the evening as he was most times. Maybe he could have talked to her—at least they could have sat and watched the waves together.

Sam got up and the boys walked slowly along the shore.

"Not having her testify must have been a relief," John said.

"It was," said Sam. "We were worried it would set her off again."

They walked on for a while. Rachel and Spy followed some distance in back of them.

"What will they do to Master Billington?" Sam asked.

John shrugged. "I don't know. Hang him, I guess."

"Here in Plymouth?"

"Where else?"

They stopped to watch a horseshoe crab scuttle into the water.

"How are things with thy father?" Sam asked.

"No change," John said with a grin. "There's little softness in the man."

As they came around the next outcropping, a small rock zipped by them and skipped across the waves.

"Oops!"

They looked up to see the governor sitting on a rock about six feet back from the shore. "Didn't see thee coming." He seemed slightly embarrassed.

"I didn't expect to see thee either, Father," John said, looking from his father to the place where the rock had skipped across the waves.

Rachel ran by them to take a seat beside the governor. She took hold of his hand. "This is our favorite place, isn't it, Governor." She smiled up at him. "John has a favorite place up the beach. Only John never skips rocks."

It was nice to hear Rachel chattering again.

She turned back to the boys. "Sometimes the governor can make them skip five times. Spy tries to chase them. He's very nice. I love Governor Bradford."

"Is Spy learning any new tricks?" John asked quickly. Talking about love with his father present made him very nervous.

"Well, she fetches things for me, but sometimes she forgets to give them back," Rachel said. "And she's learning to talk."

"Is she now? And what can she say?" Samuel asked.

"I'm not really sure," Rachel said. "She says things, but I can't quite understand her. But she'll get it right soon, won't she?"

"I'm sure she will," Sam said.

"Everything will be all right soon, won't it?" Rachel's look toward the governor was anxious.

"As right as it can be, child," Governor Bradford said.

Rachel seemed reassured, and she smiled again.

John envied the apparent ease Rachel and his father had together. The governor talked to Rachel the way he did to Mercy and Young Will, not the way he talked to John.

Spy squawked loudly and hopped down off Rachel's shoulder. "Rrrrrockkkk!" she squawked.

They all laughed in surprise, and Rachel jumped up and down.

Rachel shouted, "She said 'rock'! Did thou hear it?"

"Aye, child," the governor said as the boys nodded. "We heard it."

Spy ran down to the edge of the sea, squawking. "Rrrrrockkkk! Rrrrrockkkk!"

Rachel squealed and ran after Spy to the water's edge.

"Now say 'Rachel,' Spy," she said. "Rachel, Ray-chel."

Spy lifted her head and looked right at Rachel. "Rrrrrockkkk!" she said.

"No, no!" Rachel said. "Not rock. I'm not a rock. Say Rachel, Spy. Raay-chellll."

The bird turned and ran along the edge of the shore. "Rrrrrockkkk! Rrrrrockkkk!" she cried.

Startled by the noisy crow, some gulls took wing. "Rrrrrockkkk!" Spy called out.

"No!" Rachel yelled. "Not rocks, Spy. Gulls!"

Sam went down to join his sister.

"Rachel's getting better," John said softly.

"Aye," his father said.

John and his father sat in silence for a while, watching Rachel, Spy, and Sam. John hated to destroy the rare comfort he was feeling in his father's presence, but he had to ask the question.

"What happens now, Father? Will they hang Master Billington?" He hunched his shoulders, waiting for his father's reprimand.

"Some want to." His father answered calmly enough. "Billington himself says we ought to put an end to his miserable life. I don't know that any man would want to live with that on his conscience. But I am not sure we want to establish capital punishment here."

For a few moments there was nothing but the squawking of the gulls and Spy's and Rachel's squeals. Then the governor turned to his son.

"What do thou think?" he asked.

"What do I think?" John nearly fell from the log he sat on. He dug his feet into the sand for a better grip. "About . . ." He cleared his throat. "About hanging John Billington?"

"Aye. Are we a hanging people?"

"I . . . I don't know. Isn't that what people usually do to murderers—hang them?"

His father nodded. "Aye," he said. "They hang them for murder, for stealing, for believing, for disbelieving, for thinking, for failure to think. It depends on the place and the time." He picked up a shell and examined it. "The thing is, do we want it here, in this place, at this time?"

"I can't say, Father," John said. "I know John Billington. 'Tis different because of that. If it were a stranger . . ."

"Aye," said his father. "'Tis easier to hang a stranger." He shifted around a bit on the rock and looked directly at John. "The community will decide, and thou must accept it as must I. But it will matter, John. Whether 'tis a stranger or a friend, it will matter."

"Aye," John said. "'Twill surely matter." Again the

silence took over. All too soon, John knew, it would be time to go back to the house full of people.

With a sigh, his father left to go to a meeting. Sam and Rachel walked on up the beach together, Spy perching on Rachel's shoulder. John stayed a while, lost in his own thoughts. It was nearly dusk when he went home. There he stared for a long time at the lean-to materials piled at the outside corner of the house. Then he picked up a bunch of clapboards and wattle and headed toward the Howland house.

Afterword

This much we know:

In 1630, this crime was committed in Plymouth Colony and the man accused of the crime was hanged. Why he did it and how they knew he did it is anybody's guess. This is ours.

We do know some things that happened to these characters after 1630.

John Bradford grew to adulthood and married Martha Bourne. They had no children, but John's little brother William had fifteen children and named his firstborn John Bradford.

Sam also grew to adulthood, and after his first wife died, he married none other than Master Billington's granddaughter, Martha. Sam had six children.

Rachel lived to adulthood and married Joseph Ramsdell.

Governor Bradford lived a long and very productive life, dying in 1657 at the age of sixty-seven. He had one more son with John's stepmother. John's stepmother lived to be seventy-seven years old.

Edward Doty completed his servitude and then hired a servant himself.

Glossary

Beasthouse A building to shelter animals.

Blasphemy In colonial times, blasphemy was irreverence toward something considered sacred or held in high regard.

Bondservant A person legally bound to work for another until a debt has been paid.

Coif A white cap covering the top and sides of the head like a small hood.

Corn doll A doll made from the stalks of any grain such as rye or barley.

Doublet A man's close-fitting jacket.

Fowling piece A light gun used for hunting small game.

Freeman A voting member of a colonial community.

Froe A knife with the blade set at an angle. Used for splitting wood.

Goodwife or Goody The woman of the house. Mrs.

Johnnycake Bread made of white or yellow cornmeal mixed with salt and water or milk.

Massachusetts Bay Colony A colony of Puritan settlers in what is now Boston. Formed after Plymouth Colony.

Oldham Conspiracy In 1624, John Oldham and John Lyford wrote letters to England attempting to discredit Bradford and the governing of the church and community. They were exiled.

Palisade A tall timber fence for defense.

Pottage A dish of vegetables, sometimes with meat, cooked to softness.

Rive To split or break apart.

Rushes Plants with hollow stems that were used over dirt for flooring.

Strong water Liquor.

Trencher A wooden plate on which food was served.

Wampanoag A Native American people who lived in southeastern Massachusetts.

Wattle and daub The building material sometimes used to construct the walls of simple houses. The wattle is a rough wood framework. Daub is the mixture of mud, straw, and sometimes dung placed in that framework like plaster.

Wetu A Wampanoag house sometimes called a wigwam.